RYAN DEWEESE

WHERE RAINBOWS NEVER DIE

WARNING: Do not try any of the medical shit you read in this book. They preface the first day of medical school by telling you that half of the information you are about to learn over the next four years will end up being proven wrong through further research and study. So, best case, even if half of the medical information relayed in this story is accurate, neither of us knows which half.

rainbow: A meteorological phenomenon that is caused by reflection, refraction and dispersion of light in water droplets resulting in a spectrum of light appearing in the sky. It takes the form of a multicolored circular arc.

—*Wikipedia*

rainbow: A multicolored thing in the shape of an arch after a storm that has to do with light and water—with a pot of gold on either end defended by a maniac leprechaun.

—*Isaac Deweese, age 7*

rainbow: Hope and love.

—*Alexandra Deweese, age 10*

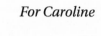

For Caroline

> *"Riches do not consist in the possession of treasures, but in the use made of them."*
>
> **—Napoleon Bonaparte**

A DESERT WALK

Suffocating heat radiated up in waves from the red-clay desert rocks during the height of a sweltering New Mexico summer. The weathered old man collected his bearings one more time and again wiped his brow with a yellow handkerchief—more out of habit than utility, because it had long ago become saturated with sweat. He had already done this trek once today. This was his second and final trip to deposit his gold. Another five hundred yards up the hill and he finally made it back to the spot he had selected to hide his hoard.

He dropped to one knee and worked the clasp that opened the seventeenth-century ornate treasure chest. The chest and the gold together weighed close to one hundred pounds which is what had forced him to make the trip twice today. First, he had brought in the chest, then he had gone back up river, and now he had returned with his backpack laden with gold. This would have been a vigorous afternoon workout for him when he was a younger man; eighty years old and weakened by chemotherapy and cancer, it was utterly exhausting. The doctors had only given him a few more months to live and he was determined to see this through.

His plan was to leave the gold here and then closer to the time of his death, he would return to lie down with his gold and die at his favorite spot in the Rocky Mountain chain. He had amassed his fortune in aeronautics after returning from the Vietnam War where he had been an accomplished fighter pilot. He was also an amateur-turned-professional archeologist specializing in Native American history and he had excavated some substantial digs in the American Southwest. So, with no family to speak of, he thought his plan a fitting end to his remarkable and storied life.

He considered scanning the area one last time before proceeding on his mission, but there was no one for miles and he knew it without looking. He emptied his backpack contents into the chest. There were gold coins, unrefined gold nuggets, emeralds, diamonds, rubies, jade, and his personal favorite item a twelfth-century Incan bracelet. He took the green bracelet in his hands and ran his fingers over it. The turquoise gemstones pulsed as if they had powerful stories to tell. He knew parting with the bracelet, even briefly, would be the hardest part of his current task. He squeezed it in his hand again before positioning it back on top of the rest of the treasure. He studied the contents one last time, closed the lid and locked the clasp, placing the chest in its final resting spot. He then took a good look around and breathed in the sweet air scented with desert pine. At this point he began his hike back through the trees and into the canyon with his empty pack slung over his shoulder. He made his way back to the river and found his waiting fiber-glass kayak, where he resumed his upriver paddle once more. He would soon return here to die in his favorite spot with his favorite relics close by. His plan was solid, but fate had other ideas...and the old man didn't die.

ONE WITH THE JUNGLE

Manco Viracocha ran through the jungle like he was one with the forest. He nimbly sidestepped sticks and twigs to avoid snapping them as he ran with break-neck speed and agility through underbrush that would give pause to the finest bushmen of today. He was late sneaking away from the fields this morning, and therefore already late for his clandestine meeting. The rendezvous was set for when the sun was highest in the sky. As he passed under an opening in the treetop canopy he paused long enough to note that the sun had already slid past its midday pinnacle. He cursed to himself and increased his pace. Leaves and branches lashed at his legs as he ran. He moved his arms ahead of himself in a swimming motion swatting them away from his face.

He arrived at his destination: a small clearing near the river. A good way downstream a waterfall tumbled eighty feet to a peaceful pool of cool, calmer water. He looked around, but the area was empty. His companion was not there. He knelt to catch his breath near the edge of the clearing with his back to the jungle, watching the river churn. The only sound was the voice of the river rumbling on, strong and stoic. He pulled deep breaths of clean air into his lungs, his muscular chest and back glistening with sweat after his run. Fifteen years old and living an active life style, there seemed not a molecule of fat on his lean body. He was in the prime of his physical life. There wasn't another sound except for the background hum of jungle noises; without warning, an arm reached out from the cover of the brush behind him and encircled his neck. He was so surprised he almost panicked. He needed to be more careful. If it had been a jaguar, he would already be dead. He tried to spin around to confront his attacker but a strong grip held him forward in the choke hold. He lunged from his squatting position, his powerful legs propelling both people off of the ground. Leaning forward, he then flung his attacker over his shoulder and into the clearing. His right hand moved for the knife on his belt, but as he looked down to strike, he noticed his attacker was female, and laughing—and beautiful. He pounced on top of her and they embraced in a passionate kiss. When they broke the kiss he lost himself in her deep brown eyes.

"You run loud," Cura said, smiling, and breaking the silence.

"And you are silent as a jaguar," Manco responded. "How did you get so close to me?"

"I know the jungle. Be one with the jungle." She laughed again. "You run like a crazed llama. I heard you halfway from the village."

He smiled at her. "Maybe so, but keep it up and I'll show you I'm also strong enough to throw you in that river."

He ran his fingers through her jet black hair and kissed the smooth skin of her tanned neck. They laid in the short grass of the clearing for some time and held each other. They had to meet discretely like this in the jungle. They couldn't risk being seen together in her city or his village. They came from different social classes and it was forbidden by law. Cura's noble blood meant she would have a husband of noble blood chosen for her someday. But today was not that day. Today was a half-day holiday so they had all afternoon to spend with each other. They swam in the river to cool off. They lay naked on the bank. They explored each other the way fifteen-year-olds tend to do.

As the angle of the sun changed and shadows formed and then grew long, they knew they needed to get back. It was too dangerous to be out in the jungle after dark. Their love was young, naïve, and blind; parting was difficult. Had they not been so teenage-love-struck, one of them might have noticed the large jaguar prints in the mud leading from the nearby river bank back into the jungle. But in the bliss of their secret affair—in the smells of each other, the small kisses, and the napes of necks—the prints went unnoticed. It was an error that would potentially carry consequences for over five hundred years to come. For, the current year was 1501, the location was the modern day Peruvian jungle at the foot of the Andes Mountains, and the Incan Empire was near the apex of its dynasty. However, in only another thirty-one years, after the empire was divided and weakened by civil war and disease, Francisco Pizarro would arrive with his band of merry men and annihilate it all.

"Genius is always bound to be misunderstood. I guess it's alright to be an asshole if you're good."

–Jason Boland

TONY STEWART

I sort of zoned out as I stood there in my scrubs and white coat, listening to the nonsensical story being laid out before me. Ten seconds into the story I knew it was bullshit. I've been a physician for thirteen years, and after just a couple you learn how to quickly tell who is sick and who just needs some attention. The fat lady continued talking and my mind found its way back to the present.

"...my belly is sore, and I haven't had a bowel movement in six weeks," she exclaimed.

"Uh huh," I mumbled.

"I don't know what I'll do if I can't move my bowels. What will I do, doctor?"

"Well, to be honest with you, we could panic—together, I mean. Let's both panic together. Or pray? Thoughts and prayers? Tell you what: you pray for a poop and I'll think happy thoughts about your poop. Or...I could get some labs and see what might be causing the problem first, then we can figure out how to move those bowels for you."

Her husband, thick bearded, equally as fat as her, and wearing a Tony Stewart NASCAR shirt, shifted his weight uneasily on his seat on the window bench of the hospital room. "She ain't shit in six weeks, doc!" he chimed in. "We want to know what in the hell you're gonna do about that. Now get a specialist in poop in here right now."

"Look," I said, "I'm a doctor. Believe it or not, I'm really good at what I do. I'm in charge of her case, and I'm telling you her bowels are fine. We can run some labs to check her thyroid levels and what not. Her bowels will work themselves out. Let's look for the underlying problem. There may be something going on here, it just doesn't start with the bowels. The bowel back-up could be the manifestation of something else that's off with her system. We have a plethora of tricks up our sleeve for inducing bowel movements."

"But I ain't shit in six weeks! I'm gonna

explode—like a bomb!" she emphasized.

And what a bomb it would be. Might level the whole building. Maybe I should just let it happen. Then I could at least go get a drink sooner.

"Ma'am, I have examined your abdomen. It's soft. It's obese, that's for sure. But it's still soft, and it's not even tender when I press on it. Frankly, it's not possible that your bowels haven't moved in six weeks. Now, I don't know what prompted you to come in today. Maybe you're looking for pain medicine, maybe you love enemas, or maybe you need a lot of outside attention dedicated to your bowels. Whatever the case may be, I do not for one second believe that you haven't moved your bowels in six weeks."

About twenty seconds of awkward silence filled the room.

Had I made my point? Had I gotten through?

Tony Stewart then stood up and took a couple steps into my personal space.

Oh boy.

"Mister, by the way you're speaking to us, it *almost* sounds like you don't *believe* her," he breathed in my face.

Holy shit.

I had to be more *direct?*

"It sounds like that because that is exactly what I'm saying. I don't believe her—at all. Her abdomen would be distended, she would be in pain, or she would be dead from the explosion she mentioned earlier."

Tony looked to his wife sitting there comfortably, then he turned to me and hissed the sweetest words a doctor can ever hope to hear: "I don't think we care to see you anymore."

Thank you Jesus. Allahu Akbar. Thank you LORD. I breathed a sigh of relief and the tension evaporated like an invisible mist as I exited the room. I had a medical student close in tow, mimicking my every move. She has a name, but I'm not sure what it is. I don't bother making any effort to remember medical students' names, so today she answers to "girl medical student." She is quite bright, though, and one of the better ones I've had in recent memory. When medical students first get onto the wards they go through these evolutionary phases. I give them more recognition and responsibility as they progress through the phases, culminating with my learning their names and teaching them something. But it starts out slowly. The first phase is the mimic phase. They stay one step behind me all day. Actually one step, and they don't know what else to do with themselves, so they copy my every move. One day I made no right turns at all. Just turned left all day to see if my student would follow me, and he did it. At this phase their responsibilities are limited to picking up my pen when I drop it. Over time they can gain my confidence and grow into tasks like getting me coffee, fixing computers, Googling answers to questions and shit like that. At a certain point, when they are competent enough and stop following me around, I'll start teaching them about medicine and giving them real responsibility. It's always a work in progress.

As a hospitalist, my patients don't choose me and I don't choose them. It's a matter of timing, luck, and happenstance that determine which patients get paired with which doctor in the hospital. So, when personalities don't mix, or the doctor accuses his patient of being a manipulative liar, it's probably best to part ways. It's a one-way street though. If a patient leaves the doctor, fine. The reason doesn't even matter. The patient can say, "I don't like white people," or, "I don't want a woman doctor," as a reason to leave. But if a doctor leaves a patient without securing any follow up or transfer of care to another provider, then it's called "abandonment." That doctor will soon be visited by someone in expensive Italian leather shoes, a.k.a. a lawyer.

So, it seems unfair. At least in this case it will be easy to get one of my partners to take over Tony's wife's care.

ANTI-DR. DIPSHIT
OINTMENT

I trudged through my day rounding on patients; reviewing charts; discussing care plans with case managers, social workers, physical therapists, occupational therapists, speech therapists, medical students, residents, utilization review teams, and insurance companies. Health information privacy my ass. The Health Insurance Portability and Accountability Act (H.I.P.A.A.) is a terrible law.

At the end of the day I can't think of eight people on the planet who don't have access to my patients' "private" health information. But if my laptop or printed patient list or cell phone is lost or stolen, or my data is deemed not secure enough, I would face reprimand. Monetary fines and even jail time are possible punishments for being irresponsible with protected patient information.

At any rate, as I'm about to leave for the day I'm stopped by my practice manager. She's forty-five, blond and always trying too hard to impress with her looks.

"Dr. Beck," she called, "I heard you had a disagreement with a patient today. Her husband says you were very rude and they don't want to see you again. I'll try to find another doctor to take over her case, but in the meantime they have filled out a formal complaint against you. A written response is required from you in eight days."

"Yeah. Ok, that's number one on my to-do list now," I shot back, my voice thick with sarcasm.

"It has to get done." She feigned too-big smile that would make a nun want to kick a puppy.

"Ok, ok, but I'll forget so remind me later," I said as I started packing my bag to leave, reciprocating a fake stupid half-smile in the process.

I dismissed "girl medical student" home for the night with a wave of the hand, and she was off before I was able to look up again. Good for her. Medical school is hard enough and any time you're dismissed it's best to just turn, run like you stole something, and not ask any questions.

I had just locked my office and was bounding my way down a dark internal hospital stairwell to the parking garage when I was jolted by the booming voice on the PA system.

"CODE BLUE, ROOM 621! CODE BLUE, ROOM 621! CODE BLUE, ROOM 621!"

In the parlance of doctor-speak, this means a man's heart has stopped and somebody who knows what they are doing should come right away and restart it. I knew the doctor on call would be responding, but I also knew that his incompetence was boundless.

At this point, I was on the basement floor, but still in the stairwell. I tossed my bag into a small recess behind the stairs and sprinted up the seven flights to the sixth floor. Several studies over many years have consistently shown that patients in hospital rooms with windows have less pain and shorter hospital stays than those in windowless rooms. Since then all new hospitals are built with the idea of trying to get patients into rooms with views. In my hospital all floors are configured in a great-big circle with the patient rooms situated around the perimeter for just that reason. And I was currently on the opposite side of the building from room 621, but I knew a shortcut. There are some administrative offices that maze around in the drab windowless interior of the outer circle of naturally lighted patient rooms. I crashed through the admin offices, bumping into someone and spilling her papers. I apologized as I rushed on, but I couldn't stop. I snaked my way through the office maze and navigated out the other side emerging right next to room 621.

I pushed my way through the tense crowd. CPR was already underway. A din filled the air in the small room bouncing off the walls and blending together in a dizzying cacophony of shit noise. A nurse was pounding away on the chest of a man who appeared to be in his early forties. *Young enough to die*, the saying goes. As I expected, Dr. Dipshit was in the corner barking out orders for things I knew wouldn't help. He was nervous and already sweating profusely—more than I was, even after my seven-flight vertical sprint.

"Doctor, we don't even have an IV!" a nurse shouted from the bedside.

I motioned to the pharmacist who had just arrived in the doorway. I made a screwing motion with my hand and she disappeared around the corner to the code-cart and came back about twenty seconds later with an I/O kit in hand. I/O stands for intra-osseous and the kit consists of a handheld power drill with a red plastic handle tipped with a long, bone-penetrating needle.

She underhand tossed me the drill. I caught it and hurried now, pushing my way close to the foot of the bed. By this point there were about fifteen people in the room and getting close to the patient was a task in-and-of itself. I examined the patient's right lower leg. There's so much to remember in medicine that we use a pneumonic to save brain space every chance we can get. *I/O-big toe*, is how this pneumonic goes.

I traced my hand up his right leg along the medial aspect until I found the area I was looking for. Just below the knee there is a triangle-shaped piece of flat bone formed by the superior edge of the tibia, the lateral edge of the tibia, and the tibial spine. This is called the tibial plateau and it ends up being the perfect spot to drill a big-ass needle into someone's bone in an emergency.

Our blood flows through our bone marrow just as quickly as it circulates through the rest of the body. So, when you need to get drugs into the bloodstream fast, and there is no intravenous access, getting a large metal drill bit into the bone marrow will allow you to disperse medications to the intended organs. In this case the heart, which had, for the moment, stopped.

I swabbed the area with a ChloraPrep antiseptic swab stick and then with gentle pressure stuck the needle attached to the drill through the skin. Upon contact with the hard bone, I squeezed the trigger of the drill. With a *zip!* sound the needle penetrated the bone and pulled its hub flush with the skin.

I removed the drill from the needle, unscrewed the cap off of the I/O needle, and attached a short piece of IV tubing. The whole endeavor took me about twenty-five seconds.

"I/O access is in," I announced. "Get ready to give epinephrine one milligram with the next pulse check."

During the pulse check, while the epinephrine was being pushed into his bone marrow, and the nurses were switching compression roles, I moved the bedsheet off of the patient's other leg. It was massively swollen compared to the right leg, into which I'd just inserted the I/O.

I tugged on the scrub sleeve of the curly-haired blonde nurse beside me. "What's this guy here for?" I asked.

"Chest pain and shortness of breath," she said. "He was supposed to have a cardiac stress test tomorrow morning."

"Did they ultrasound this huge leg?" I inquired.

"No, I don't think so," Curly Hair replied.

My mind was racing now. This guy was young enough to die, but not on my watch I decided. As CPR continued, I pushed through the crowd over to the pharmacist. She was legit and, like me, sort of unorthodox in that she cared more about patients than scripted protocols.

"The leg is really swollen. This guy has a blood clot that has moved from his leg and lodged in the large vessels exiting the heart. He needs TPA. He needs the clot-busting medication. It's his only chance. Go draw it up. Go now!" I told her.

"Dr. Beck, you know it's not in the protocol," she said. "They'll never let you give it."

"He's dead. His heart has stopped. He has ceased to be," was my retort.

"It's worth a shot," I then pleaded.

"Even if I draw it up you're not going to be able to convince anyone to give it," said the pharmacist.

"Just draw it up? Please? He looks like he's about eighty kilograms for the dosing weight."

She disappeared around the corner to her medication cart to draw up this guy's only chance at seeing tomorrow.

Someone from deep in the shadowy depths of the room yelled, "Time?"

"Ten minutes since we started compressions," came the faceless reply of the code record keeper from a recessed corner of the room.

I fought my way back through the crowd to plead my case with Dr. Dipshit.

"Hey, man, this guy's got a pulmonary embolus.

Look at how swollen his leg is," I said.

"I don't think so. I admitted him earlier today. Seems like coronary disease. His history was very consistent with a cardiac source of chest pain," he replied.

"Come on, history isn't everything we go off of. Plus look at his leg!"

"I didn't notice the leg," Dipshit responded after a slight hesitation, glancing down at the swollen flesh.

"We need to give TPA," I exclaimed. "It may help even if it's a coronary blockage."

"No! It's not in the protocol. It won't work, and he would have a high chance of bleeding to death."

"Well, he's already dead, so I think he would want us to try."

"No."

"You're going to let him die?" I asked. "You're not even going to give him a chance?"

"I'm going to follow the evidence-based protocol that gives him the best chance of survival."

"Your evidence is only as good as your statisticians. If you're good enough with numbers you can shape the evidence into anything you want. You can't pigeon-hole these patients into your protocols! Every one of them is different." I tried some emotion in my voice, but it was to no avail.

"No, and actually, get out! I'm on call! I'm in charge! What are you even doing here? Go get a drink you lush. OUT!" he added for emphasis.

Our exchange drew a couple of uneasy glances from some of the other staff in the room. I glanced up at the rhythm on the monitor during the ongoing pulse check. There was evidence of electrical activity in the heart but no pulse. This was a pulmonary embolus. I decided what I needed to do. I took two steps around the curly-haired nurse and this maneuver put her between Dipshit and me. By this time the pharmacist had made her way to the bedside opposite me.

The TPA had been drawn up and was in the breast pocket of her white coat. I stretched across the bed and plucked it away from her. Quite powerful stuff for such a small amount of liquid. It makes the blood extremely thin and inhibits all clotting for a time. This would either break up his clot and save him—or finish him off with an internal hemorrhage, most likely in the abdomen or the brain. I hooked the syringe onto the I/O access port and depressed the plunger, infusing the medicine into his bone marrow.

Dipshit saw me as I started the push, but with the curly-haired nurse in between us he couldn't get to me in time. When he reached the bedside he ripped the syringe out of my hand and disconnected it, but not before I got all of the medicine in.

His face displayed his shock. "What the hell are you doing?"

"Saving his life," I shot back. "Now just give me five more minutes of CPR to circulate the medicine."

"His heart has been stopped for close to fifteen minutes. I'm gonna call time of death here," he said.

"Give me five minutes," I demanded, our eyes locked in icy stares.

Everyone in the room had stopped and was looking at us.

"Two minutes," he said, his voice oozing with disgust and disdain. "I'll give you one more cycle of compressions and breaths. If there's no return of circulation at that point, we're calling it."

One two-minute cycle of CPR is five rounds of thirty chest compressions followed by two rescue breaths. Two minutes is only one hundred and twenty seconds, but this turned out to be the longest hundred and twenty seconds of my life. I watched the second hand on the wall clock and the heart monitor. My eyes darted back and forth. After the fifth cycle the compressor paused for a pulse check. Two nurses were checking either side of his neck for a carotid pulse, and two more had a hand in his groin feeling for a femoral artery pulsation.

One of the nurses looked up and smiled. "We have a pulse!"

Dr. Dipshit scowled and shoved his way out the door.

Boom Baby! I thought, as I called out some further instructions, "Run a blood pressure, bolus two liters of lactated Ringer's solution, send a rainbow panel of labs, check a STAT EKG and a STAT echo."

As the nurses began scurrying about in all directions, either executing the orders or heading back to their regular posts, I slipped out and made my way back to the stairwell to retrieve my bag. I contemplated the long drive home. It was a fifty-minute drive from the hospital to my loft. It was also sixty miles. I drive fast. I once made it from my loft on the north end of Indianapolis to downtown Chicago in two hours flat, but that's a story for another time. I had just one more stop before I could head to my Jeep and go home for the night.

GOOD LUCK - BAD LUCK

Emily was six years old when her father drank and drove one time too many. He had the whole family in the car. They were coming around a curve on the interstate when the traffic in front of them stopped on a dime. Sixty-five to zero in an instant. Not enough warning for anyone, really, let alone a drunk guy. The collision had been horrendous. Her mother and father died instantly. Her little brother was ejected from the vehicle, across the interstate, and into oncoming traffic. The authorities later pieced together that his car seat had been improperly installed. He had no chance even if he had survived the initial impact.

Emily though had somehow survived. She was knocked unconscious but came to as the firefighters used the Jaws of Life to pull her out of the heap of twisted metal that had previously been a car. She was rushed to the hospital where the emergency room doctors diagnosed her with a mild traumatic brain injury, an epidural hematoma, seven broken ribs, a hemothorax, a broken femur and in a cruel twist of fate—something much worse. Her CT scan discovered a mass on her kidney: Wilms' tumor.

Emily had never had any kind of a home life. She had grown up in Charlestown, Indiana where her mother had spent her days doing meth and ignoring her children. Her father worked odd jobs and performed the occasional shady smuggling job for the Kentucky Mafia. He was perpetually drunk and neglected to ever show his children any love. He was often violent with their mother and that violence had once bruised Emily's face. Her parents had missed the kindergarten sign-up period and she had not yet started school before the accident. She had also missed routine checkups which negated any chance of the palpable kidney mass being discovered early.

She had no surviving family to support her. Both sets of grandparents were dead. Emily's uncle, her father's brother, was alive but serving a lengthy prison sentence nearby at the Wabash Valley Correctional Institute in Carlisle, Indiana. Emily had never met him. Her entire immediate family perished in the crash. Therefore, the State of Indiana awarded custody of her to one Tiffany Keams.

Emily had been a permanent hospital resident for the past three years, already outliving her doctors' survival projections. She had forged headlong through agonizing rounds of chemotherapy and radiation, including the typical accompaniments of hair loss, weight loss she could ill afford to lose, and the relentless nausea, vomiting, and diarrhea.

Wilms' tumor is one of the more curable childhood cancers. Early detection and therapy is now responsible for an exceptional cure rate. Stage I, II, and III disease can be cured ninety-five to one hundred percent of the time. That is, as long as the histology is not anaplastic. Anaplastic histology refers to how mutated the cancer cells appear under the microscope. This takes the cure rate down below thirty percent. With Emily's late detection and extreme anaplastic histological state her chances of survival were very poor indeed.

The long odds, the hair loss, and the vomiting and diarrhea did not affect her personality though. She was a delightful little girl and was adored by the hospital staff. It didn't hurt that she was charming, painfully cute, and always smiling. She had formed close bonds with some of the nurses and other staff as well.

HOPE IN A POEM

When I got to her room after my duel with Dr. Dipshit, she was spread out on the cold, white-tiled floor, studying a detailed map of the Rocky Mountains. The map had rivers, lakes and elevation all listed. It was an adorable sight to see a tiny, cute kid pouring over a map with the same focus as a surveyor would.

As usual, she had her stuffed owl under one arm. It was white and soft and squishy. The owl's face was arranged in a professorial expression complete with a monocle over one eye.

"Thomas!" she exclaimed, as I entered the room.

She was weak and tried to get up off the floor, but I knelt down beside her instead and leaned in for a hug.

"How's my favorite person in the world today?" I asked.

"A little weak. More chemo starts tomorrow," she replied, the smile disappearing from her face.

"How's Hootie?" I inquired, motioning to the owl under her little arm.

She thrust the owl into my chest for his obligatory hug and I complied.

"What's all this?" I asked and gestured toward the maps laid out on the floor. "Are we moving west?" I roused.

"There's a treasure out there!" Her blue-green eyes sparkled and came to life. "Some old archeologist hid about two million dollars' worth of gold somewhere in the Rockies when he thought he was gonna die. But he didn't die! And so he left the treasure there and wrote a poem full of clues to help people find it."

"And you think you can find it?" I asked with a laugh.

"No, but you can."

"I think the chemo destroyed too many brain cells this time," I said, raising one eyebrow at her.

"Hey, I've been looking this over, and I can't figure it out." But then her adorable little face lit up. "But you can do it. You're the smartest person in the whole world."

"Uh-huh, yeah right," I replied.

OUT OF TIME

I knew why she was looking for treasure. She was running out of chemotherapy options. Her cancer had returned twice now, and if she failed the next high-dose attempt there was one option left and it was a longshot. There was an experimental drug called Doxybutex that had shown some promise in animal testing. It was a silver-based chemotherapy. We couldn't get our hands on it, because at this point it was still in experimental animal trials and not approved by the FDA for use in humans. Time and time again the state Medicaid medication approval office had declined her petition to receive it. It carried a high price tag because it was still in trials and wasn't being mass produced.

Emily, meanwhile, still sat innocently in the background of this play and was running out of time. Twice we had appealed for insurance coverage and twice we had been turned down. The estimated price of making enough for a thirty-kilogram girl would be just over $750,000. Emily was an especially bright nine year old. She was aware that her chances of survival were limited at best and getting worse each day. I assumed she was looking for the treasure to fund her experimental chemotherapy—her last chance at life.

"That crazy old man didn't hide any treasure. He just wants fat American kids to get off their asses and get into the woods to experience nature," I poked.

Emily twisted her cute face into a scowl and glared at me.

She shot back, "He has no reason to lie, and I've read all about it. Lots of people think that it's real. He's a war hero, a pilot, and an archaeologist. And we also both have cancer of the kidney. If he already beat it then maybe I can too."

She got up and started a pitiful shuffle toward her bed but got tangled in the web of IV tubing and wires that continuously monitored her heart rate, respiratory rate, and oxygen saturation. I unhooked and untangled some of her wires and got her back into bed before hooking them back up. I got her tucked under some blankets and situated as best I could, at least moving the wires away from her face.

"Scooch over a little," I said as I lay down next to her. "What is it tonight? Chris and Kim get eaten by a wolf pack? Or is it Chris and Kim die a horrible death in the Amazon jungle?"

"Neither! It's *Magical Adventures of Chris and Kim: Discovery of Atlantis*," she said.

Despite never having had any formal education, living her first six years of life with abusive parents, and her next three confined to hospitals, she was teaching herself to read and doing a good job of it. I helped when I could, and Tiffany did a lot with her. Plus, she was always cajoling a nurse to read to her. Right now she was enthralled with the *Magical Adventure* book series. The two main characters are brother and sister: Chris and Kim. They discover a magical book that transports them into the story to that time and place that they are reading about. After completing a mission and helping someone in need they narrowly escape certain death by reading a chapter set in the woods near their house in Oregon and they are transported back to safety in the nick-of-time. They just have to say the phrase, "Take me there."

"Ok, where were we? Chris and Kim were

swimming under the ocean looking for Atlantis," I said, adding something about thinking the big water would win this one. She clutched her owl, Hootie, to her chest and rolled her head over to one side.

I read chapter nine, and she quickly fell asleep.

I gently closed the book and slipped out of the bed. Looking at her sleeping peacefully and thinking about the totality of her situation was paradoxically poetic, and beautiful, and heart-wrenching, and unbearable all at once.

INTIP CHURIN

Inti was just waking. Even his earliest soft morning rays were a welcome relief as they helped beat back the cold Andean mountain night. A happy Sun-God made for happy crops, and if they could get at least a little rain everyone would be happy. Inti was the most important of all the Incan Gods. The Incan people referred to themselves as *Intip Churin*—children of the sun. Manco raised his hand to his face. He wiped the sleep from his eyes and kissed the ornate green and gold bracelet that adorned his left wrist, a permanent fixture ever since it had been given to him years ago. Other than memories, it was the only thing he had left of his family. His parents had died long ago. His mother had died during his birth. His father had died in battle, fighting to conquer new lands for the great expansion of the Incan empire. In their culture, children were wealth and yet his father had ever had only one wife. It was a polygamous culture and he had always been welcome to take more wives and have more children, but he had explained to Manco that after knowing his mother he would never love another again. So when Manco's father was selected from the fields to pay his *mita* and serve his required enlistment as an *aucu* warrior to help with the Incan conquest of new lands, he had pulled his son aside and given him the bracelet that had been handed down in their family since its creation four hundred years prior. His father had told him the story of the bracelet, that it had been blessed with special powers and that as long as he had it with him it would keep him safe from harm. Manco had never taken it off since donning it that day.

And his father never returned from war. An honorable death in battle serving the empire is all he was told. He should be proud they told him. Because of his father's sacrifice and bravery the Incan empire spanned from modern day Ecuador down the vast expanse of the Peruvian coast, east to the Andes

Mountains, into Bolivia and Argentina, and south reaching to southern Chile. These facts, at the time, provided little comfort to a grieving boy with no family.

Other cultures throughout history would have put the orphaned boy in the streets or sent him into the military to die in service of his empire at too young an age. But the Incan social safety net was quite advanced for the 1500s. For the most part, they took care of their people. There was a class system, yes, but orphans were taken care of and the boy had been taken into an orphanage. He worked as a farmer in exchange for food, shelter, and even a chance at an education. He worked hard. He helped his foster mother with the younger children. He led in the fields. And he had aspirations. The Incan class system was unbreakable but not necessarily unmalleable. Incan royalty was bloodline. Men who were not of Incan royal blood lines were called *yanca ayllu*. However, through education, study, and service to the empire, even an orphan could eventually follow a long path to become a member of the royal class, not by blood but by "privilege." Then and only then might he be allowed to marry his Cura who was already of royal blood.

Manco's orphanage was made in the typical Incan architectural style of stone walls with one small trapezoidal door and a grass thatched roof. The grass was thick and good at keeping the rain out but there were no windows. The central fire place had no chimney and the inner walls hung dark and heavy with generations of black soot.

Inti peeked over the top of the mountains and a couple of early rays sneaked through the one door of the house and found their way onto his face. Manco shivered. Looking down from the raised wooden sleeping platform in the center of the room, he noticed the fire had gone out. He gently kicked awake the ten-year-old who was supposed to have been watching the fire.

"Vala. Wake up. You let the fire go out," he said in their native language of Quechua.

"Oh no! I fell asleep!" the boy exclaimed in a hushed whisper as others were still sleeping. They both sat up. "I'm sorry brother. I'll get more wood and get it started again. I don't want you all to freeze."

"It's ok," Manco said giving the boy's shoulder a reassuring squeeze. "It's morning. I will help you."

They laid the fireplace with some wood and dried out llama dung used for burning. The house wouldn't need the heat for the day, but their mother would need the fire for cooking the two meals of the day.

While Vala blew softly on the embers of the new fire, Manco stepped out of the house and surveyed the expanse of gorgeous mountains around him. To his disappointment the ground was still dry. No rain had come overnight again. He looked to the west. There were no dark clouds in sight. The rain god, Illapa, was not listening to their prayers. It appeared the drought would continue for now. The priests would be getting nervous if rain didn't come soon for the thirsty crops. And nervous priests were not fun for anyone.

He shook off the thought. Breakfast was cooked in a pot over the fire. Corn mash with diced peppers blended in for spice and flavor. Eight orphans sat on the ground outside the front door of the house while their foster mother ladled the mash into clay bowls and passed them out.

"Crops are struggling with no water," one of them said.

"Even the irrigation ditches are dried up," another responded.

"It's been a month without rain."

"What have the priests requested for sacrifice?" someone asked.

"Daily devotions from each of us. Whatever you can give. And more prayers."

"Tomorrow five of our most precious black wool llamas are to be tied up and given no water. Surely Illapa will hear their cries of thirst and bring the rain we need."

They finished their food and Manco, being the oldest, led their *ayllu*, or family group, to the assigned fields to be tended for the day. The fields they farmed were steps cut into the side of the mountain rising up one steep tier at a time. This technique, invented long ago, made cultivating the steep rocky Andean hillsides possible. Dirt was mounded up then flattened and braced with a rock wall, leading higher and higher up the hillside. This allowed the new areas of flat land to be worked and farmed, and also if rains did become heavy the leveled steps kept crops from being washed away down the mountain. The group followed Manco up the hillside to begin the day's work.

MILK BLOOD

I finally made it to my Jeep and out of the hospital. On the way home the day's events replayed in my mind as the white line of the road zoomed past me. After reliving it all I kept coming back to one thought that I couldn't shake. I didn't know what I would do without that little girl. And while her death grew more likely each day, even the hint of the thought of it made me shudder. I know death. I thwart death on most days, begrudgingly accept it on others and occasionally welcome it with open arms when that is the best outcome for my patient. But not with her. She was different somehow. Life was trying to cheat her. She deserved more. She deserved better. She deserved a chance at life. I felt deep down that, if she could survive, she would be destined for something great. I felt she was meant for something more.

As I reached home, I made my way up the sixteen industrial steps flanking the side of the old warehouse leading to my empty loft apartment. I stood on the landing and fished in my pockets for the keys. As I searched, I came across a scrap of paper in my front breast pocket of my scrub top. I came in and went straight for the bar cabinet. I poured a double Johnnie Walker Black and downed it in one swallow. I tossed the keys and the scrap of paper onto an end table and poured another drink. I don't own a television. I pulled some History & Physical papers from my bag that "girl medical student" had written that day and sat down at my aged and creaky wooden kitchen table to grade them.

It's not a grade, per se. It's more of a subjective assessment of medical competence and giving some pointers on how to not kill patients when you graduate and don't have a supervising physician looking over your shoulder anymore.

For her first H&P she had collected an excellent history. She had all the right elements that the insurance companies require. Pertinent to the situation or not, the insurance companies require a review of the patient's social, family, and surgical histories in order to submit a bill. The diagnosis had stumped her though. The patient in question was thirty-six years old and had come in with abdominal pain. She had a vast array of electrolyte abnormalities discovered on her initial lab work up as well. Her sodium was extremely low at 116, potassium was low at 2.1, and chloride was off. My student's differential diagnosis, as we say, included: dehydration, small bowel obstruction, appendicitis, and anorexia. I knew the answer, and it wasn't on her list. The phlebotomist or the nurse or whoever had drawn the blood must not have called my student. I pulled my laptop over and logged into our electronic medical record through remote access. I clicked on the patient's chart and was able to pull up a note from the phlebotomist. There it was, just as I suspected:

"Blood obtained from the right AC. Highly viscous. White," it read.

White blood. It looks like heavy cream when you draw it up. Severe hypertriglyceridemia. The genetic defect causes too many lipids to be made. The body and blood become saturated with it and the result is a triglyceride level of 1,500 when it should be 150, and blood that looks like milk. One of the frequent complications of this is irritation and inflammation of the pancreas, i.e. pancreatitis. Ergo, the source of this patient's abdominal pain.

I hoped "girl medical student" hadn't tried to fix all of those out of whack electrolytes. Those were false values. The viscosity of the blood in someone with this disease is extremely high. The machines the lab uses to check the electrolyte levels can't process this thick milk-blood and all the reported results are falsely low. You could kill this patient if you saw that falsely low potassium level, didn't put the whole picture together, and were aggressive in your attempt to replenish her potassium levels.

I called the hospital and told the nurse to hold any potassium orders for the night. I'll give the medical student some education in the morning. One nice thing about the practice of medicine is my student will never miss this diagnosis again because patients have faces. So going forward, every time my student sees an electrolyte panel that is off in every facet and milk-blood, she'll remember this patient's face and get it right.

HOPE IN A POEM: REPRISE

I got up and refilled my scotch with a triple. As I poured from the crystal decanter, I noticed the paper I had found in my pocket lying on the end table. I took it over to the couch with me and flopped deep into the cushions. I took a long pull of scotch and unfolded the paper. It was a page torn out of a magazine. Someone had written in the top right corner.

"Thomas, you can find this treasure. You're the only one who can do it. I believe it in my heart. Love, Emily."

The article detailed the story of Donovan Dean

and his famous poem, a poem he claimed left clues to a hidden treasure worth a couple million dollars. The poem was included in the article, too:

The truths of the treasure
Come to One who is bold
Who is called down under
WeT and cold
ApprOach the souRce
Through the flow of the flood
To stay afloat
To stay above
Then come upon
The sOund made like thunder
Where paths are crossed
As the Meek shall waNder
The mark below
The eyes of the owl
Under the call
Of the biG cat's wail
Seek the treasure
Laid quickly down in the wOod
When all is answered
As dreams only could

I studied the poem trying to envision the old man stashing the treasure box somewhere in the Rockies.

Where would he hide it? Where would I have hidden it if it were me? Imagery from the poem and visions from my imagination combined in my mind in brief flashes. But they were incomplete. My eyes got heavy as I continued to daydream. I had a vision of running my hands through a pile of gold coins. Five A.M. would come pretty early, I knew, so I downed the rest of the tan liquid in my glass, stretched out on the couch, closed my eyes and welcomed the escape of sleep.

THIRST

Today, as most days, they worked happily. Inti shone in the sky. He rode higher than the clouds, proudly ruling over his domain. His rays bounced off the Incans' brown skin depositing some welcomed warmth. But the crops withered. The drought was taking its toll. The potato leaves sagged and hung limply. It was obvious the corn was suffering and thirsty as well. There was much work to do. Manco and his foster siblings pulled weeds. They mended broken sections in the stone retaining walls. They fertilized the corn and potatoes. They found what little water they could in the nearly bone-dry irrigation ditches and hand-watered the gods' share of the crops. All their fields were divided into thirds. The best third was reserved to sacrifice to the gods and these fields were tended first and given the most attention and care. The next third was set aside for nobles and royalty; it was tended, watered, and fertilized second. The remaining third was the food for the commoners and it got whatever fertilizer, water, and care was leftover to give in each day.

Midmorning, one of the younger orphan's *taclla* broke. It was a wooden bronze-plated plow that goes on the foot for turning up the dirt. The boy was upset.

"It's ok," said Manco. "Go gather more wood stacks for the fire for tonight." Then, on his hands and knees, he finished the boy's work for him. When the sun was halfway between its pinnacle and its end of the day surrender, Manco called out for everyone to return home. They ate a dinner of *locro*, a potato stew, seasoned with more diced chili peppers, and tended to chores around the house before bed.

SHARP - DRESSED MAN

At the five A.M. chime on my phone I rolled over, still a little foggy from the alcohol of last night. I dragged my ass to the sink and splashed cold crisp water on my face. As I looked in the mirror I wondered how long I could keep doing this to my body. I was thirty-eight and felt much older. Between the torturous hours of medical school, internship, residency, then being new to practice and working to establish myself, and now with heavy drinking my body had grown sick of the beating it took on a daily basis.

I felt like a 1978 Chevy pickup truck with

rusted-out floor boards and 200,000 miles on me. No time now for feeling sorry for myself, though. I took a small dab of Cremo brand shaving cream and spread a thin layer over my face, neck, and head. I flipped open the straight razor with a flick of my wrist and began to scrape off the stubble in long steady strokes. Fifteen minutes later I was shaved, showered, and out the door. Head shiny, smooth, and reflective. I chose to wear a suit today. Day in and day out, scrubs were the norm, but I just had an instinctual feeling today should be a suit day. I had chosen a good-fitting, light-charcoal suit, and a starched white button-down accented with a thin pink tie that ended squared at the bottom. Pink was Emily's favorite color, and with any luck I would also run into her state-appointed guardian, Tiffany.

And luck was on my side. I parked the Jeep in the hospital garage, and there, pulling in at the same time, was Ms. Tiffany Keams, the most beautiful creature I had seen, or would ever see in my life. High cheekbones framed her pretty face and her tan skin reflected her Native American ancestry. To a fault, she sometimes wore too much eye shadow, which I loved.

"Hi Tom! Good morning. Why the suit? Very sharp. I didn't know you cleaned up at all, let alone so well," Tiffany greeted me.

"Hi Tiffany. I just like to look good for you. And

how are you today? I see you're looking lovely as ever," I responded.

"Oh blah." She dismissed my compliment with a wave of her hand. "I came in early to check on Emily. When did you see her last?"

"I saw her last night. I put her to bed before I left the hospital. We read a *Magical Adventure* book and she went to sleep. Why?"

"The nurse called me early this morning. I guess she had a bad night. Sounds like she was up all night with chest pain and trouble breathing. You know she's more prone to developing blood clots because of her cancer. They think that's what she has. She's in the CT scanner now." Tiffany's voice betrayed a slight quiver.

Oh no, I thought. *What's with me and pulmonary embolism the last couple days?* PE was treatable if it wasn't massive and immediately fatal, like the code patient's yesterday could have been. That wasn't the big problem. Emily would just need twice a day injections of enoxaparin under the skin. My concern was that with an underlying cancer like hers, it only takes one small setback like this to trigger a cascade of bad things, often leading to a patient's death.

I came back to reality, but didn't let my inner worry show. "OK, let me check on some things and I'll meet you in her room after she's out of CT"

"See you then," said Tiffany as we parted ways.

MOGWAI

I made my way to my office, threw on my white coat, and clipped my badge to the lapel. I draped my stethoscope around my neck, and logged onto the computer to print my patient list for the day and do a quick check of morning labs and vital signs. At first glance, everybody on my list looked pretty stable. I ordered a unit of blood to be transfused on a guy, and ordered some replacement potassium for three people who had gotten a little low. Then I opened Emily's chart to see if her CT scan had been read by the radiologist yet. No luck. "In Progress," is all it said. I badged out of the computer and headed down the stairs to the radiology department to see her scan for myself.

On my way to the stairwell I had to pass by room 621 and, as I did, a woman grabbed me by the arm to stop me.

"You're Dr. Beck! I'm Margaret Langford," she said. "My husband is in room 621. I heard what happened last night. I had gone home to freshen up and get some rest, but the nurse told me he's alive because of you."

As she said these words, she began to sob.

"Thank you. Thank you." She said it again and again, like she couldn't ever say it enough. "You don't understand. He's my everything. I can't live without him. You saved us both." She pulled me in close for a tight hug.

It did feel good to get a little recognition, to get a thank-you that is often deserved, but more often skipped over in the daily chaos of my profession. I reflected in the moment that this was why I had gone into medicine to begin with. This was why I had sacrificed my twenties. It was for the human connection. It was for a chance to make a difference in someone's life. It was for the chance to help someone when they are at their worst. However, due to the business of medicine and the current state of healthcare this is also the part that is first to be trivialized and marginalized when things get busy and times get tough. And when it is pushed away enough it often leads us to question why we ever went into medicine in the first place. My eyes misted a little as she hugged me. I wiped the tears on the sleeve of my white coat and told her she was welcome. She thanked me again as we parted.

I made my way down to the basement where all the radiologists are kept like where you try to keep family members you're ashamed of when company comes over. They work in dark windowless rooms hoping the world won't be able to see them for the freaks that they are. Note: Important safety tip. These weirdos almost never see the sun, so if you do ever encounter a radiologist on a sunny day, stay a safe distance away. Especially don't mix alcohol with the sunlight.

They're kind of like Mogwai. The right combination of sunlight, alcohol, and keeping them up past midnight can turn them into Gremlins. It usually ends with an expensive bar bill, a paternity test, and/or a lawsuit. I know from experience.

"Hey yo!" the radiologist said as I entered his darkened cave of a reading room.

"Hey, Martin," I said.

It was so dark, it always took my eyes about twenty seconds to adjust. I stood just inside the doorway and waited for things to come into focus. Martin sat in front of three large high-resolution computer screens and the hum of the machines filled the room with background noise. Martin himself was dirty and fat and had a brace on nearly every joint on his body. His work station looked like a two-year-old's highchair with crumbs and jelly smudges everywhere. There was an open jar of peanut butter on his desk and a six pack of Diet Pepsi near his feet. He had to have either banished the environmental services team from cleaning his work station, or more likely they had given up on trying to keep it clean, filing it away as a lost cause.

"Can you pull up Emily's scan?" I asked.

"Sure. What are we looking for?"

"She had chest pain and shortness of breath last night. We want to rule out PE"

"Can do," he chirped. Then his mouse started clicking away to pull up the right scan.

As the black and white images loaded on the screen, we sat in silence. Black and white is a little misleading because the whole principle of the CT scanner is to project different body tissues onto the screen in varying shades of gray that are based on each tissue's density. The machine can create the image with about a thousand different shades of gray to help the radiologist distinguish blood from bone from tumor, for example.

The images loaded and Martin scrolled through them with his sticky mouse wheel until he found what he was looking for.

"Aha. There we go," he said. "Right main pulmonary artery has a large filling defect. There are multiple other scattered smaller right-sided emboli as well but this large one just off of her heart is the big worry. Poor kid. She's not gonna end up making it is she?"

"I don't know anymore, Martin. I don't know."

That clot burden was substantial. I'm no radiologist and even I could see it there on the scan. This was not good.

"OK, thanks man," I said, turning to go.

Martin stopped me as I was leaving. "Hey Tom?"

"Yeah, Martin. What is it?"

"I heard you were drinking again. I just want to make sure you're not drinking too much, that's all," he suggested.

"Thank you, Martin, but I always drink just the right amount for the situation at hand," I replied, stepping back out into the blinding light of the hallway, which is like stepping out onto the surface of the sun.

CANCER AND CLOTS
AND SHOTS

I went to her room right away. Tiffany was already at the bedside. She was holding Emily's small hand. A myriad of wires crossed Emily's body and Hootie was wedged under her left arm. I checked the numbers on the bedside monitor. Blood pressure was good at 110/55. Heart rate was elevated to the 140-150 beats per minute range, which was to be expected with a large pulmonary embolus. The concerning thing to me was her oxygen saturation, which was only at ninety-one percent. It was okay in that it was in the low end of the acceptable range but she was using five liters of oxygen per minute through a nasal cannula to maintain it. She must be putting a tremendous strain on her heart muscle to maintain a decent oxygen saturation with that large of a clot burden.

I moved in close to the bed and sat down next to Tiffany. I rubbed Emily's lower leg and she smiled. For the briefest moment, my left hand brushed against Tiffany's right which caused us both to freeze for an instant. I dared not move, savoring the contact until she pulled away, sneaking me a quick glance that I caught from the corner of my eye as she did so.

I noticed the heparin infusion pumping into Emily's arm from the IV pole and our eyes met. When Emily looks at you, I mean really looks at you—it's a deep look. You seem to be able to see into her soul, and you can see that there is nothing phony about her. Everything is genuine. She also seems to see your soul as well. She sees the truth and there's never any point in lying about anything when talking to her. That was the case right now when our eyes met and she asked me the question I had hoped to avoid.

"Thomas, I don't feel very good. Will I survive this?" She whispered this over the hissing flow of the oxygen. Her words stung like daggers.

Again, painful as it was, there was no point in lying to her. She would see right through it.

"This is not what will kill you." Instinct took over and I just went with the truth. "This is a big setback though. We just have to give you a blood thinner. We start with the heparin infusion, but we should be able to switch to enoxaparin injections twice a day and you can get off of this drip soon."

"Oh, more shots? I hate shots," she moaned.

Tiffany caressed Emily's head and started crying. The scene was tough for me as well. Here were the two people in the world that I cared about the most. One I even loved for sure. My thoughts were cloudy and I felt vulnerable. I didn't like the feeling and it made me leave the room and go for a walk.

I walked down the hallway and got a coffee from the machine with some change I bummed from nurses along the way. When I returned to the room, Tiffany was breaking more bad news to Emily.

"Baby, I know you don't like shots, but that's not the whole story. With your blood clot and new increased oxygen needs, the doctors say your body can't tolerate any more chemotherapy right now," she said.

"So I just die?" Emily asked with a flat face.

"No baby. Chemo is just on hold until you get stronger. Then you can start it again when your body is ready."

"Oh, you mean when the tumor is larger and has

spread more throughout my body?"

Like I said, she's a bright kid.

Both of them began sobbing again. I took Tiffany by the hand. I didn't notice I was crying until later when I tasted the salt of my own tears rolling down my cheek touching the corner of my mouth.

"I don't want to die. I don't want to be buried in the ground. Please don't put me in the ground," Emily begged. "I'll get dirt in my mouth and have to taste the dirt. I never want to taste the dirt."

1120 COMMON ERA

Cancha felt the end of his life nearing. It was more than a feeling, a sensation. His fever was high but he wasn't in pain. He just knew his time in this life was running out. That's why he worked furiously, consumed by the project at hand. He was not scared of death. Death was welcome. He only feared the timing of it. He feared the thought of not finishing the piece of art he had spent a great part of his life creating. While he had made countless pieces of jewelry in his lifetime—it was his tradecraft—he had put his soul into the piece he was working so hard on now. He had been slowly and methodically pouring over each minute detail of it for the last twenty years. And if you'd have asked him, he could not have told you why. He had felt compelled by some unseen force to do it.

The materials he used were the finest. He had used fine threads of gold and copper. The silver for the band was the purest he had ever laid his hands on. The turquoise emeralds had been collected over many years from different *huaca*, holy sites, and during holy times. Even amongst those superior stones he had selected only the best and then cut them flat to lay flush in the inlay of the silver bracelet. Bands of thin copper tied the stones together and held them in place in the inlay for extra security. Gold threading accented the ornate etchings on the sides. It was his most prized piece of art. And now with his death looming, he felt compelled to see it to completion.

He worked through the day and night and day again. He became weaker and his fever peaked higher. As he neared the end of his task on the evening of the second day of his illness, he sent for his friend. When his old friend arrived it was dark. Cancha lay close by the fire, shivering and sweating at the same time. The light from the flames danced around the small room, occasionally lighting up a face or a darkened corner. The bracelet was complete but the artisan was near death. He struggled for air. With his last dying effort he gifted the bracelet to his dear friend.

"There is a power in this adornment. Take it to the *Villac Uma* and see what prophecy is foretold for its future. We will see each other again in another life, old friend."

And so the bracelet was passed on to Hatun, the eighth great-grandfather of Manco.

SAFE IN A SUIT

It was turning out to be a long twelve-hour shift. Most of it was spent on my feet. My mind was distracted by Emily's situation but it flipped back and forth between the little girl and the satisfying way Tiffany's soft hand had fit into mine. Luckily, most of my patients were on cruise control that day whether waiting for their antibiotics to work on their pneumonias, or waiting on insurance companies to approve their pending nursing home stays. No one required me to use my brain much, and it's a good thing too, because I may not have been a lot of help had a patient needed me to think critically.

I had just finished rounding and dictating discharge summaries when I got a text from the practice manager summoning me to our department chairman's office. It was a small, shitty, windowless office situated smack in the middle part of the middle floor of the hospital.

If you thought the office was bad, you definitely wouldn't like the attached administrative position. I felt sorry for the guy who had the job. For no extra money, actually a slight pay *cut* due to lost production, and just the reward of a line item title on your resume, or the chance of further advancement up the administrative ladder, he was supposed to corral, cajole, inspire, and support a cast of thirty doctors into daily excellence and improvement. And since we are dealing with doctors here, independent thinkers who don't like to be told what to do, this guy might as well be trying to herd cats. Few professional groups are so independent-minded, autonomous, and set in their ways as physicians.

When administration wanted a new quality measure emphasized or a new treatment protocol agreed upon, it was always a struggle to get physicians to agree to new or standardized ways of doing things—or to change at all for that matter. And this was the sucker charged with getting our free-thinking group to conform.

It seemed to be taking its toll on him too. When I arrived he looked like hell. His beard was long and untrimmed with too many flecks of gray for his age. His hair was disheveled, and he seemed to have gained another five pounds every time I saw him.

I knocked on the door to his tiny office and he barked for me to come in. I made an awkward squeeze into one of the two frayed chairs facing his cheap aluminum desk. The other chair was already occupied by the practice manager.

Oh, boy. This should be fun, I thought.

"Dr. Beck, welcome. Look, I know you're busy," he started in right away. "We've got a couple of things we need to discuss. We had a complaint from a family member about your bedside manner with his wife. He alleges that you were rude and didn't take her complaint of constipation seriously. Do you remember this patient?"

"It was all nonsense," I defended. "No bowel movement in six weeks? Come on. She would explode. Besides her abdominal exam was normal. Belly was soft, not even distended."

"Could we not approach it with a little more tact?" he asked. "When a formal complaint like this is filed, we require you to submit a written response and the complaint goes in your permanent file."

He leaned back and his worn-out swivel chair interrupted him with a squeak. It looked like it was from a thrift shop. "Anyway, that's not the main reason you're here. An incident report was filed about you running a code last night and not following the ACLS protocols—or any hospital protocols for that matter," he continued.

"The patient is alive. His wife thanked me in the hall today," I responded.

"That's not the point. If he hadn't lived she would sue us, you, the hospital and the system. She would sue everybody. The code blue committee has called an emergency meeting for tomorrow morning. They want you there at seven A.M. to tell your side of the story. The CMO, the CEO, and the quality officers will all be there."

"I can't believe this! I saved his life. He was dead. He had to be resuscitated. We should call him 'Jesus,' he's so resurrected, and yet I'm in trouble!" My voice was rising a little.

"This is a serious one," the practice manager chimed in. "We both know your file isn't spotless. You were on thin ice before this. You could be facing suspension."

I felt safe in my suit for some reason. I felt professional. Had I not had it on I might have snapped and destroyed the whole matchbox of an office. Maybe burned the building down. Instead, I stood up, and buttoned my top coat button as I squeezed past the corner of the desk and out the door. I had the sudden strong urge for a drink.

"Seven A.M. Don't be late," the practice manager chided me.

I did not look back.

HIT SOMETHING HARD
I DON'T WANT TO LIMP
AWAY FROM THIS

When I got home, I tossed down my keys and went straight for my decanter of scotch. I downed the first one and then I saw the piece of paper Emily had given me the day before. It was right on the couch where I had left it. I picked it up. It was the poem that supposedly led to the old man's treasure. Then in a decision that would sculpt my life going forward, in a moment which would mark my life and the lives of others in ways that I could not yet see—I put the paper in my pocket, went to my medicine cabinet, opened my pill bottles, and dumped them all in the trash can.

The next day I awoke on the couch. My phone was buzzing but I couldn't seem to locate it. My hand followed the vibrations past two empty scotch bottles and between the couch cushions to grab it. As I sat up a bit, I noticed my head was pounding like someone was stabbing me with a knife in the left temporal bone of my skull, each throb corresponding to a heartbeat. I put the phone to my ear.

"Go," I said.

"Where the hell are you!" screamed my boss, much too loudly for any compatibility with my headache. "You missed the meeting! You missed any chance to tell your side of this story!"

"I missed the...What day...Oh is it past seven?" I asked.

"It's two o'clock in the bloody afternoon!"

OK, that was enough screaming for me at this point. In my flattest, most insincere voice, I said, "I'm sick."

"Sick! You couldn't let me know? You could have called, texted, emailed, sent a carrier pigeon. Plus, you don't sound sick!" he screeched.

"Yeah sorry," After thinking about it a second longer, I just hung up the phone. There was a joke about being "sick enough for you" that crossed my mind, but it would have to wait for another time. I noticed seven missed calls and twelve unread text messages. As I was swiping them off of the phone, another text came through.

"You are suspended without pay until further notice."

I tossed the phone onto the coffee table and dropped to the floor on my hands and knees. I crawled to the kitchen and opened the bottom cupboard where I found my friend, another bottle of unopened Johnnie Walker Black, and I twisted off the black cap.

THE ANCIENT GREEKS
KNEW SOME SHIT

In the medical community, bipolar disorder used to be officially called manic depression. Long before that, the ancient Greek philosophers had already more accurately coined the terms "mania" and "melancholia" for those whose moods seemed at times to be too high and too low. They even noticed that if the affected person bathed in water heavy with lithium salts their moods seemed to balance out a bit. Typically, the brain of an affected person oscillates between periods of dark depression and periods of elevated mood. The severity of the mood elevation is known as "mania" or "hypomania" based on the intensity, and sometimes the presence or absence of hallucinations. The episodes of mania are manifested by lack of a need for sleep, feelings of grandeur, abnormally high energy levels, and impulsivity. Occasionally, great creativity and hypervigilant thought processes accompany these manic periods for some people.

I had always been prone to tip to the manic side of the scale. I had my episodes of debilitating depression as well, don't get me wrong, but my natural inclination was toward mania. As a creative person already, any throw into mania for me was a period of potentially tremendous glory, as the manic brain would see it. Now, no longer tethered to a middle ground by the lithium pills that I was supposed to take twice a day, my brain was free to unlock its full potential. And unlock it did. With only mild-to-moderate collateral damage.

PROPHECY

Hatun, saddened by the loss of his oldest friend, one whom he had played games with in childhood and fought alongside in adulthood, did as his friend had requested. He made an appointment with the high priest to have divination performed on his valuable gift and a prophecy foretold about its future. On the morning of the set appointment, Illapa had unleashed a great storm that shook the mountains to their core. Lightening blistered the morning sky and ice-cold rain soaked the ground like a saturated sponge. A bone-chilling wind blew hard out of the west.

Such trivial inconveniences though did not postpone an appointment with a high priest. Hatun, with the bracelet adorning his wrist, haltered his finest llama and set off on foot for the temple. The climb up the mountain road was a struggle against the wind. He felt the weight of it heavy against him. The rain lashed at his face and chest. The llama was a hindrance as well. As if sensing its impending sacrificial death, it fought Hatun stubbornly the whole way. After three hours he arrived at the foot of the steps of the temple. He was met by the high priest who led the way up the many steps to the temple's flat top where the sacrificial stone awaited. It was there where the llama was to be killed and offered up as a humble sacrifice to the gods in exchange for the prophecy reading of the bracelet.

Together Hatun, his llama, and the priest ascended the steps higher and higher. Slowly and deliberately they climbed. The storm raged on, violent across the steep steps. Low storm clouds hung nearly upon them now. Lightening still crackled all around them. At last they reached the top of the temple. The priest pulled his knife from his belt and set his footing as he prepared to slit the llama's throat. As he did so, his foot slipped on the wet stone and he fell down. In falling, he dropped the knife. It clattered on the stone. They both looked on as it skittered to the back edge of the terrace and down into the depths of the jungle below.

The priest looked up in astonishment. He turned to Hatun.

"Without sacrifice there can be no prophecy today," he said in a deep and serious tone. "Come back tomorrow."

Just then the wind surged violently and the clouds parted in a large circle over the temple. The rain over the temple stopped. Inti showed his face and bathed the temple in sunlight. A large brilliant *huanacauri*, or rainbow, formed across the expanse of the sky. It was the largest anyone had ever seen. It seemed to stretch from one border of the kingdom to the other. The priest turned to Hatun with a quizzical look on his face.

"Come forward," he commanded.

Hatun walked toward the priest as he was ordered.

The priest took Hatun's hand in his and examined the bracelet in detail. He held it up to the sky. The light from Inti glinted off it in every direction. The priest then held it toward the rainbow. Each of the colors poured into the bracelet and then magnified back off of it in a dazzling ballet of reflected, dancing colors which projected onto the surrounding lands. The priest dropped Hatun's arm. He extended his arms straight out in front of himself with his palms up and stiffened his back like a board. He began to pray out loud. Several minutes later when he was finished he turned back to Hatun.

"The gods have spoken. No sacrifice is needed today. Your llama will live. This bracelet is blessed. It will protect the innocent forevermore, as long as it is possessed."

THE MAN IN BLUE

When Tiffany found me two weeks later it looked like a bomb had gone off in my loft. I was determined to catch that rat bastard today. I'd noticed he appeared every day except Sundays dressed in blue with a large tan satchel. He'd throw letters and bills and papers and magazines and medical journals in the black box on the wall beside my door. To get there though, he had to climb the sixteen stairs that ran parallel to the warehouse up to the landing outside my door.

Today his reign of terror would end. I had loosened the bolts on the railing of the landing and removed the screws from one of the deck boards as well. As he stepped on the loose board his balance would shift to the right. He'd be forced to lean on the railing close by and the rail would give way. My nemesis would topple to his death, bringing balance back to the Force.

I waited, peering through a window from behind a blind. It was about eleven A.M. when he came walking up on this day of reckoning. As he approached the steps though, he slowed his pace. It looked as though he was studying the scene. I had moved some of my potted plants so as to funnel him into my ambush. As he pondered the odd plant arrangement on the landing he caught a glimpse of me peering through the blinds.

Drats, he must realize trouble is afoot, I thought.

"I'm not coming up there, you psycho!" the mail carrier shouted toward the stairs. "I don't know what you have planned, but I'm done with you. Yesterday you shot me. You shot me!"

His description of said events was true, but incomplete and therefore inaccurate. I *had* shot him, but only with a BB-gun, and only from some distance, and only in the ass. I'm a crack shot with my BB gun, after spending my formative years under the tutelage of Uncle Bruce.

Realizing that my plot had been uncovered, I burst out the front door. I was shirtless with two stripes of black face paint, one under each eye, pink boxer shorts, Teva sandals, and was holding an antique wooden golf club. In my haste to jump out the door I planted my own foot on the loose board, and unable to slow my momentum, hit the railing with all of my weight. The loose bolts popped out of their holes and the railing tipped over the side. The railing section was light though and I was able to kind of throw it to the side as I was falling. I barely managed to catch myself on the concrete slab where the rail had once been with my other hand. It clanked to the ground with a terrifying clatter as I hung from my fingertips.

"You bitch!" I yelled back at the man in blue at the top of my lungs. "I'll get you tomorrow."

"Hey pal, I'm not coming back, and you're a psycho!" he shot back. "Get some mental help, shitbird!"

I hung there for a several moments. As I began to have thoughts of pulling myself back onto the landing, an apparition of a beautiful woman hovering over me appeared. As the image came into focus it spoke; I realized the woman was real.

"What in the world are you doing?" Tiffany exclaimed as she extended an outstretched hand. "And what are you wearing?" she asked with a quizzical look on her face.

I pulled myself up onto the landing with her help

then moved past her in my pink boxers. She followed me into the flat.

"Here." She placed a stack of mail on the entry table.

"No, the man in blue? Did he get to you too?" I asked, worried, taking her by the shoulders and looking her over.

"You mean the mailman?" she responded, looking confused and shrugging my hands off. "He gave me your mail and said you were trying to kill him."

I sat down on the couch and started pouring over some more plans and sketches I'd laid out detailing different ideas of how to stop the rat bastard. Tiffany looked around and the enormity of the situation began to sink in for her. The loft was in total disarray. Clothes were everywhere, empty scotch bottles were stacked in a great pyramid against the back wall. It fell just short of reaching the ceiling.

"Oh, my God. You're off your meds," she exclaimed when she put it all together.

Then she examined me more closely. Our faces came in close proximity to each other, as if she was studying a specimen in an alien zoo.

"You're rail thin! You've lost so much weight! When was the last time you ate?" she asked.

"Three days, seven hours, and sixteen minutes ago." I knew it down to the minute.

"Slept?" she asked.

"Two weeks, two days, and exactly five hours ago." I knew that down to the minute as well.

"And what's that smell?" She kept her line of questioning going. "When was the last time you bathed? Never mind, I do *not* want to know that. Where are your meds?"

I returned my attention to my plans, and without looking up, pointed toward one of the trash cans that was overflowing with garbage.

"OK, here's what we're going to do," she said matter-of-factly. "First things first, I will dig through this mess and find your meds. You're going to take them, and then we will get you in the shower and wash away that awful smell."

She rummaged through a great pile of rubbish until at last she found the pills at the very bottom of the trash can. She handed me two different colored ones. "Here take these." I tried to wash them down with a scotch that I had out on the table but she took my glass away and handed me a water bottle she had brought in with her. I scowled, but swallowed the pills with a swig of water.

"Now you shower. Clean yourself up and then we feed you," she said.

"How did you find me?" I asked.

"I know where you live," she replied.

"Why did you come?"

She paused.

"Emily misses you. It's been over two weeks since she has seen you."

"Ah, yes, the girl." I smiled now as I spoke. "How is she?"

"She's improved a little, but still on oxygen. Could be permanent." She paused and looked at the ground before speaking again. "Tom, they say there are no further chemo options. They are consulting hospice tomorrow."

"Well, no worries there," I responded spritely. "That won't be necessary."

"What do you mean?" she asked.

"Have a look for yourself."

I waved toward the bedroom area of the loft as I went back to my sketches and plans for mailman termination. The bedroom of the loft sits about two steps higher than the rest of it, and it is set back in one corner. At the time, it was only separated from the rest of the loft by a simple curtain. As Tiffany pulled the curtain back, she gasped at the sight before her. The walls were covered, every inch, with maps, diagrams, copied pages of old museum filings, Native American quotes, and pencil-scratched GPS coordinates on scraps of paper. In the center of one wall, above the head of the bed, was an enormous map of the Rocky

Mountains with a single red push pin in it.

"Tom..." her voice betrayed her confusion, unsure of what she was seeing. "What is all this?"

"Oh that? Yeah, I found it," I responded, still pre-occupied with my plans on the coffee table.

"Found what, dear?"

I walked over and stuck my head around the curtain.

"I found Donovan Dean's treasure. I just have to go get it."

THE BETTER YOU SLEEP, THE BETTER YOU EVERYTHING

After I washed off two weeks of accumulated stench in the shower, Tiffany took me out to a local ramen place. My appetite made a rapid reappearance when hit with those delicious aromas and I ate two bowls. The warm, salty pork broth and vegetables, with a soft-boiled egg and seaweed on top seemed to nourish more than my abused body. Ramen had always been a food that nourished my soul as well as my stomach. Much to my dismay, we passed on the beers and stuck to waters as

I walked her through an abbreviated decoding of the poem and how it would take us to the treasure. She was skeptical at first, but the more into it we got the more convinced she became. I zoned out at the table a couple of times during the meal, partly lost in her almond eyes, symmetric dimples, and jet-black hair, and partly because over two weeks without sleep was catching up to me. My medicine and the warm broth in my stomach was slowly returning me to some semblance of a stable mood. Tiffany drove me home and, after removing several stacks of books and maps from my bed, she was able to tuck me in under the covers. I got a smile and a peck on the cheek and I was asleep before she even made it to the curtain on her way out.

BLINDED BY THE LIGHT

The drought continued and Manco kept at his work. He led his *ayllu* into the fields each day for the rest of the week. At the end of it there was to be another secret meeting between him and his love in the soon-to-be style of the Capulets and the Montagues. On the appointed day, he worked double time during the morning hours and his brothers and sisters agreed to pick up his slack in the fields in the afternoon, so he was able to slip off at noon and meet Cura again in the jungle clearing. Her embrace was warm and welcoming, and her lips were soft and sweet.

And for lounging in the blinding light of love—today they would begin to pay a heavy price. Last week they had missed the jaguar foot prints in the soft mud near the river, but the jaguar had not missed their scent upon their return.

JOHN - BOY

I awoke nearly twenty-four hours later, rolled out of bed, and found my phone. One missed call and voice-mail caught my complete and undivided attention.

"TB, this is John-Boy. Answer your phone, man. It's here. Thanks goes to me and only me. It's the chance of a lifetime, baby. Pack your bag. Pack your clubs. We're going to play Pine Valley."

John-Boy is a way-back friend of mine. We grew up on the same street. Well, basically the same street. Our houses were separated by exactly two and a half miles but only three turns, and in the backwater county in Southern Indiana where we grew up that's about as close to growing up on the same street as you can get. We were instant friends the first time we met. We were the kerosene that fed each other's flames. However, I would quickly learn that being friends with John-Boy had its price. He was bright and a couple of years younger than me. He'd followed me to medical school, but that road proved too long for his patience and he dropped out. He was always working a different get-rich-quick scheme and he always seemed to drag me with him from one mess to another.

It started with hustling kids at poker for their lunch money with a deck of marked cards. As with all of his schemes though they either didn't work, or the hustled caught on and didn't return, or sometimes caught on and returned only to physically beat his ass. Sometimes my ass as well. As he grew up, the hustles evolved and became more involved, more elaborate. The card playing morphed into ways to try to cheat in online poker rooms. Then came attempts at counting cards at blackjack on midnight runs to dilapidated Indiana river casinos.

Hustling pool, hustling bowling, hustling golf— he would even play chess for money. John-Boy was always looking for a quick win, and always ended up a quick loser. He had been somewhat successful at golf, not on the hustler scene, but just in general as a golfer of his ball. And, like always, he had dragged me with him. We played a lot of golf growing up. When we were eight and ten years old our parents would just drop us off at the local golf course every morning during summer break and come back to get us when the sun went down. We had played so much that by the time we were college-aged, we both had full golf scholarships. I went on to play for Texas and John played for Georgia.

Lately, John had turned his efforts to the business world. He had found a cushy job that afforded him the time to get his MBA online during the downtime at work over the course of a couple years. He then made a little money on an insider stock tip and now his eyes were seeing dollar signs again. His plan was to conquer the market by starting his own investment fund. He secured a business partner from the financial sector and was arranging meetings all over the country in an effort to raise investment capital. John-Boy was nothing if not ambitious. His frame was tall and he was handsome and lean. Perhaps his most distinguishing feature was his sandy brown hair which contained a small but prominent patch of bleach-white hair on top of his head. I told him he looked like that sister from *Frozen*.

"It's a mark of destiny," he used to tell me.

Destiny for greatness or destined to end like a Greek

tragedy? was the unanswered question that came to my mind every time someone brought up the patch of white hair.

And now he might be getting us on Pine Valley. As anyone who's ever picked up a golf club knows, this was a once-in-a-lifetime opportunity. My fingers couldn't punch his number into the phone fast enough.

"John-Boy," I said when he answered on the first ring.

"TB, pack up," he ordered.

"What are you talking about? How in the world did you set this up?" I asked.

"Steel," he said, like that was an actual answer.

"What?"

"Steel. So, I'm going around the country soliciting investors for the fund and I hit it off with Abe Smith the founder and owner of ABG Steel Corp. They are the second largest steel manufacturer in the country. He says he likes me, says something I said struck a chord with him, says my white hair streak is speaking to him of luck. He's thinking of investing in the fund but he wants to get together to hear a little more over golf at his club, which happens to be Pine Valley. I can bring a plus one and you're my Huckleberry."

"When do we go?" I asked.

"Tomorrow. Southwest has a six thirty A.M. flight

out of Indy to Philly. The course has a shuttle that will pick us up at the airport."

"Tomorrow! That's pretty short notice, and kind of a lot's happened since we last talked," I said.

"It's Pine Valley, man—once in a lifetime," he said.

I did some quick calculations in my head.

"Let me make some calls and I'll call you back in five. Oh and by the way, what's the catch?" I asked.

"No catch."

"John-Boy, with you doing the planning, there's always a catch."

I hung up and called Tiffany to check on Emily. Apparently, she was still in good spirits. They were setting her up with a large oxygen tank for home and she was getting used to it. Tiffany was at the hospital and handed Emily the phone.

"Hi Thomas! Where have you been? I haven't seen you in weeks!" she exclaimed.

"Oh, I've been catching up on some work from home," I said. I was unsure if I should tell her about my discoveries regarding the hunt for the treasure yet. In reality, it was unlikely she would ever see it now that her prognosis had worsened with her oxygen dependency and blood clots.

"They say I may be able to go home with Ms. Tiffany on Monday. I don't mind the oxygen. Sometimes I pretend like I'm an astronaut. The tank even has a good spot for Hootie to ride. I made him a little basket on the top of the tank and he rides there just watching me. I take him on walks twice a day. Everybody here loves it," she said.

"What *Magical Adventure* book are you reading?" I asked.

"*Polar Bear Cub on the Loose*!" she responded suspensefully.

"How are Chris and Kim going to get out of that one?" I asked.

"Well they know now never to get between a momma bear and her cub. They also got to see the Northern Lights which sound amazing."

"Seems like an adventure," I said.

"And, if they don't get eaten by this momma bear, and they can just make it back through this blizzard and then they say the magic phrase, 'Take me there,' they will be transported back home."

"Sounds dangerous. And cold! Get some rest. You have the big adventure of coming home soon yourself to deal with. Love you. Let me talk to Tiffany again."

"OK, I'll see you soon."

"See you soon," I replied.

Tiffany took the phone and stepped out into the hallway.

"Hey, she's OK?" I asked.

"As good as she can be I suppose. You know the

vitality and blind optimism of youth," she replied. "I want her to get some extra rest this weekend before I take her home on Monday. Let's give her some space this weekend and try not to get her overstimulated about the transition. Plus, if you're not around it will give her nurses and the rest of the staff some more time to say their goodbyes. Do you think you could just wait until Monday and see her at my house? She gets so excited when you visit and I think she would get better rest if you stayed away until Monday. And you're OK now as well?" she asked.

"Oh yeah, I'm getting back to normal. Thank you for coming over and getting me back on my feet. And I understand about the weekend. I was going to maybe get out of town anyway. I've been cooped up in the loft for so long...."

"I think it would be good for you to get out and get away for a couple days. A short rebalancing, if you will. Catch your breath. You've been through a lot lately. We'll be here when you get back," Tiffany said.

"Good advice. Maybe I'll play a little golf," I replied, with one side of my mouth curving into a smile.

"Just remember to take your meds," she added.

"In," read the one-word text that I sent to John-Boy. I stood up and started packing, wondering if I would even be able to find my golf clubs in this mess.

YOU WILL NEVER
PLAY HERE

The stretch of strip malls, gas stations, and fast-food joints that lines this state highway in New Jersey is indiscernible from countless others like it in the state—and around the country for that matter. That is, except for the fact that this one is home to a small discrete entrance to the top-ranked golf course in the country. We crossed the railroad tracks and eased up to the understated guard house with a lone elderly guard on post. He identified the Mercedes van that had, forty-five minutes earlier, picked us up at Philadelphia International Airport, and waved us through onto the hallowed grounds of Pine Valley Golf Club.

What started out as 184 acres of pine barrens had been purchased in 1913 had now expanded to 623 acres of golfing paradise, the brainchild of hotel mogul George Arthur Crump. It's almost magical to leave the urban landscape you're so immersed in, cross the tracks, and be transported somewhere indescribably special. It's as if time in this place stopped, or never even existed.

The exclusivity is remarkable as well. If you Google "Pine Valley" one of the first articles that comes up is titled, "You Will Never Play Here." There are believed to be just under one thousand members worldwide. The list of names—a closely-guarded secret. Ever since Mr. Crump set out designing the unique layout from scratch, it has been a haven for a select few and a mystery for everyone else.

Marshlands had to be drained. Tens of thousands of trees had to be cut and the stumps removed by horse and chain. This made way for the massive movement of sandy earth that majestically ended up joining the natural beauty of the landscape with one man's savant-like vision to become the masterpiece that it is today. What Crump couldn't finish before his death in 1918, was thankfully taken up and seen to completion by Harry Colt and Charles Alison.

We turned in and crossed the seventh fairway and pulled up to the simple but elegant clubhouse where we were greeted in a cul-de-sac by the caddie master and the pro.

"Brooks Blackburn. Welcome to Pine Valley, Dr. Beck. We've been expecting you," the pro said as he extended his hand for a warm and vigorous shake. "You gentlemen are meeting Mr. Smith. He just called ahead. His companion had an emergency cancellation so I'll be playing with you to complete your foursome. The porter will show you to your rooms where you can change. We'll meet down here in the dining room in thirty minutes for lunch."

I was shown into the clubhouse, mindful to remove my hat indoors per club policy, and up to my room just down a small hallway off of the locker room on the second floor. The whole clubhouse has a simple charm. It smells of old wood, not musty, but seasoned. It smells like—history. We were led up a narrow creaky staircase to the locker room. The lockers are simple white-painted metal cages which afford no privacy to the contents. On one end is the shower area, sinks, and stalls. There are no women allowed and it has a bit of a fraternity feel. There are no doors to the bathroom area, no doors on the toilet stalls, and no doors or curtains on the shower stalls.

Each shower, though, is a piece of heaven in its simplicity and frugality. Naked pipes bring water to an overhead rain shower the size of a manhole cover. Being under one is like standing under a waterfall, and if you don't drown, all of your impurities, stresses, and worries are sure to be washed away along with any of the light brown sandy soil from the course that may have stuck to your skin from the round.

The other end of the locker room leads up two steps to a narrow hallway lined with eight individual sleeping rooms. Again, each is beautiful and perfect in its simplicity. A single queen bed anchors each room with a thick dark-red bedspread embroidered with a Pine Valley logo on the corner. There is a corner chair, a small mirror above an aged wooden dresser, and a simple lamp in the corner between the bed and the chair.

After looking around and inhaling a deep breath of the air of such a historic place, I did a quick change into golfing attire and made my way back down the stairs. The stairs exit between the pro shop to the left, and the great room to the right. The great room is also home to the bar, and that was my first stop. I'd had three drinks on the plane already, but nothing since we landed and I was getting thirsty again.

"Dr. Beck." The barkeeper already knew my name as he welcomed me. "What can I make for you, sir?"

This was some service. I'd been on property all of ten minutes and the entire staff probably already knew my name. Heck they probably knew every guest's name before they even set foot on the property.

"Scotch, please. Johnnie Walker Black. Kiss of water."

"Sir, we are extreme top-shelf-only here. The cheapest I have is Johnnie Walker Blue."

"I like this place more each second. Sounds great. Make it a double."

"Make that two doubles," John-Boy said, clapping his hand on my shoulder as he came up beside me and bellied up to the bar.

"Can you believe this place?" he remarked.

"No," I replied, "and what's even more amazing is that *we're* here."

"OK so Mr. Smith is flying into Canada County airport. It's a small airfield near here where he can land his private jet. We're going to play Mr. Smith and the pro, Brooks Blackburn. Smith's other guest couldn't make it. We'll do business at the last minute, after we've won him over with our charm."

"Big money game?" I asked.

"You know it," John said with a wink.

"Alright, if I'm gonna play well I need some nourishment."

THE FRENCH LAUNDRY
IS JUST ANOTHER
LAUNDROMAT NOW

Drinks in hand, we headed for the dining room which was located through the bar and off of the great room. I was still a bit emaciated from my manic break and my shorts were about to fall off me. I was cinched up to the first notch on my white Puma belt. Some good food would sit well. But I had no idea what I was about to experience. Little did I know, "good" was not an adjective that has, or ever has had, any place in the Pine Valley dining room. I would find out later that the joke goes they built the Pine Valley Golf Course so the members would have something to do in between meals. The food is outstanding, lip-smacking, knee-wobbling, toe-curling delicious. We started with the turtle soup topped with a splash of sherry out of a logo-emblazoned decanter from the center of the table. A plate of the best coleslaw you'll ever have is also served to each table as an appetizer. We finished our drinks and they were refilled.

The menu had about eight items on it and each description looked spectacular. Mr. Smith arrived and joined us as did Mr. Blackburn. I choose the chef salad which ended up being a brilliant mix of lettuces and herbs tossed and topped with a split soft-boiled egg, home-pickled carrot and radish slices, and thin-shaved aged French white cheddar. There was a full six ounces of thin-cut wagyu beef seared to rare, and it was all splashed in a house-made vinaigrette. John had lamp chops with a reduced balsamic vinegar glaze. Mr. Blackburn had already eaten and settled for a drink called a Frandsen: half lemonade, half grape juice. Mr. Smith never looked at the menu and ordered a grilled sea bass sandwich with baby arugula and goat cheese. Had he glanced at the menu, he would have seen that dish was not on there, nor were any of the ingredients he ordered. The waiter jotted it down, said, "Very good," spun on one foot, and was gone.

The table conversation centered on Mr. Smith.

"John tells me you're in steel?" I asked him.

"Second largest steel manufacturer in the country. Built the whole company with these two hands," he told me, as he held up his giant paws for me to see.

They bore heavy callouses and you could picture him down on the factory floor, making sure things were done to his specs and expectations. The rest of him was stocky. He was strong, but a good deal overweight, I guessed by about fifty pounds. What drew you to him were his eyes. They were a piercing gray-blue. He came across overall as formidable. Not to be taken lightly, but still likable. As I studied the deep lines in his facial features, I noticed three small whitish plaques on his skin, two under the left eye and one under the right. Xanthomas, otherwise known as cholesterol deposits. It was an often overlooked sign that the cholesterol level in his blood was too high. Definitely a risk factor for heart disease and stroke. *Whichever number wife he's on, could be the lucky one,* I thought cynically.

John went on to talk about his company and provide a little more background. The food arrived and was everything we could have wished for. As we finished, we set the terms of our match. Five hundred per hole, per man, with automatic two-down presses. In a game with those stakes it would be easy to win four or five thousand dollars. But as we got to the first tee, it turned out John had one more gem to drop on me.

BLACK SOCKS

There's only one sign on the first tee of the greatest golf course in the world. There's not even a sign designating that you're on number one tee. The sign they do have simply reads, "No Mulligans." As we walked over to look at it, John pulled me aside and whispered, "By the way, Doc, I need you to lose."

"What? Why the hell did you make the stakes so high then?" I protested.

"He needs to win. He'll be happier and more likely to invest if he wins," said John.

"You son-of-a-bitch, you're going to cost me

about six grand."

"Yeah, but just invest with me and you'll get exponential returns later and then you can thank me."

"I'll take my chances on the lottery before I give you a nickel."

"We'll see. Thanks for coming by the way. Enjoy your round."

Mr. Smith and Mr. Blackburn walked up with caddies in tow. Good lucks were wished all around and a tee was flipped that pointed toward me. I stepped up and piped a driver about 280 yards with a high cut down the middle following the right-hand dogleg of the fairway and we were off.

It's important to know that the best course in the world is also one of the hardest. The fairways are wide but often command some shaping of your tee shot to get in the best position. The green complexes are large but can be made lightning fast. They have a great deal of slope to them as well, which can add to the speed and treachery. If you miss a fairway or a green the punishments are severe. There are about eight hundred bunkers on the course I would guess and in total—zero rakes. So, if you end up in a sand trap it's usually a difficult lie and truly the punishment it's intended to be for your misstep. It's also certainly not the soft snow-white powder with perfect texture and consistency that pampers tour pros today. The caddies at Pine Valley are excellent. Range finders are discouraged. Most shots involve significant elevation change so it's easier and faster to just trust your caddy when he tells you how far to fly it.

Off of number eight there's a halfway house that stocks a generous array of snacks and drinks. By the time we hit that point John and I were up three holes, or up three and one with the automatic presses if you speak the lingo. The halfway house has a large wall covered in a golf ball rack where any logoed golf ball you want to donate will be displayed. Across from that is a bar. There are some beer bottles on display, two beers on tap, every type of candy bar ever made since America became her own nation, and thank God, Scotch whiskey. I got a triple on ice and perused the golf ball display while John waited on a draft beer to foam down.

"Nice playing," John said to me. "You're one under, right?"

"Yeah, I think so," I said.

"OK, time to let them back in it."

"You're a shmuck."

"Come on. Listen. I have the matrix. The matrix that I made can correctly predict the success of biotech startups eighty-five percent of the time. I just need some capital to get the fund started and we can make it big this time," John pleaded with me.

"Alright. Alright," I grumbled. I was picturing myself counting out stacks of hundreds and handing them over begrudgingly after this round. I turned back to study the wall. Lots of logo balls stuck out. I noticed the big Indiana schools—IU, Purdue, Notre Dame, and Butler. There were balls from some of my favorite courses in America: Palmetto, Victoria National, Wolf Run (R.I.P.), Briggs Ranch, Dormie Club, Arbor Links, Ballyhack, Hidden Pines, Crooked Stick, and even my home club Holliday Farms. But one in particular caught my eye. It was low on the rack, and the logo featured an off-white barred owl with big dark eyes. Below it read "National Audubon Society." I thought of Emily and Hootie and how much she would like that ball.

By the time we reached the par three tenth hole we had managed to lose the ninth to a birdie from Blackburn, making our bet up two and even. After looping just a couple holes with me, my caddie knew my yardages like his own. So, the tenth, with a middle pin today was 161 yards actual but played about four yards downhill so about 157 yards. He tried to hand me the nine-iron thinking that would put me just below the pin on this steeply pitched back to front green, and leave an uphill look at birdie that would be reasonably makeable. Instead, I reached in the bag for the pitching wedge.

"Sir, don't think the pitch will get there today. Best hit the nine," he told me.

"I think you're right, but the pitch is what is called for in this situation," I said, nodding towards our playing opponents.

The caddie gave me a knowing nod and I could see that he understood how this was going to end. Blackburn hit first just right of the pin to about ten feet. Mr. Smith hit it a little long onto the back of the green, leaving a nasty slick downhill putt for birdie. John pulled it long left on the back fringe leaving a difficult putt as well. I addressed the ball, gave a deep shoulder turn and made good contact just for show, knowing full well I stood no chance of getting to the green with the wrong club in my hand. The ball rose to the apex of its flight arc and plummeted out of the sky. Then, in an odd defiance of physics, didn't bounce but instead seemed to sink deep into the depths of the earth. I had found the infamous Pine Valley bunker of legend, The Devil's Asshole.

The Devil's Asshole is basically the scariest bunker imaginable. If you've ever played golf or even seen it on television, that's all I have to say is "scariest bunker imaginable." It's almost a pot bunker but there is just enough room to temp you to try to take a full swing. It's so deep and steep that there is a wooden staircase that takes you down inside the eight-foot deep hole after your mistake. The bottom, where the ball comes to rest, is scalloped out so that it's not flat but steep on all sides leading down to the ball, so you can't get under it at all. You can barely even get a club down to it. As I stood above the mess I'd made looking down into the asshole like a gastrointestinal doctor about to perform a colonoscopy, my caddie handed me my fairway rescue. That seemed odd. Typically I hit it low-ish and about 230 yards, however, I needed this one to go *super* high and about ten yards.

I looked at the club, then at him, then back at the club, then back at him. "You're nuts," I said finally.

"It's the only chance, sir. Open the face and hit it as hard as you can into the right face of the bunker and it sometimes pops out," he said.

"That's our plan, eh? Sometimes it pops out?" I asked.

Well, I had no choice now. And I'd had worse plans myself from time to time. I ambled down the steps into the colon. It's so narrow down there that it was all I could do just to get a swing on the ball. I still have nightmares about it. The ball smashed into the front wall of the bunker just a couple feet in front of my face and caromed upward. I lost sight of it for a moment against the bright sky then heard a thud on the earth...*behind* me. I turned and the ball had traveled backwards and landed over my head. I worked my way out of the asshole, with a little dirt or sand or shit or whatever on my face. I chipped it up on the green, made the bogey putt to save some face, and we lost to a par from Mr. Blackburn. I made a mental note to gut-punch John-Boy as soon as we were alone.

With my caddie now on board for our lay-down, it was much easier moving forward. We made it look more realistic. He would misread a putt for me on purpose or give me a yardage that was off just enough so I'd end up in a difficult spot. We ended up losing three and two and one for right at $3,000 per man. I know John well enough that I'd brought cash. My vision of counting out and peeling off hundreds came to fruition. We squared up bets in the porch area off the back of the clubhouse while the bartender delivered more drinks. Aside from the payout, it was a beautiful thing. He didn't ask me, just delivered a double Johnnie Walker Blue on a big spherical ice cube in a highball glass. John stayed away from alcohol because of migraines but in the social situation of a business deal he was trying to close, he was allowing himself to imbibe. He had a mojito muddled with mint fresh from the chef's garden.

Mr. Blackburn went to tend to some business in the shop and Mr. Smith was starting to lighten up after two mint juleps and an extra three grand that he didn't need in his pocket.

"Can you believe this?" he asked. "This is my favorite spot on the planet. I've been coming here for fifteen years and there's no place I'd rather be."

"I heard you came in on your own jet. I guess the steel business is good?" I asked.

"The company has two Cessna Citation XLS jets. I use one mostly for myself. Short answer is, yes, the steel business is good. I could jet down here for the day and be back in New York for dinner if I wanted. But, as you gentlemen can tell from lunch I hate to miss any meal here if given the chance."

"John here says he's about to corner the biotech market and make a stack. Let's get you on board and we'll donate the Cessna to charity and put you in a Gulf Stream G-550."

"Hey, if it were only that easy." He laughed and reached for his drink.

The bartender came back out with a tray of fine cigars and another round of drinks. We each chose a cigar as the conversation continued. There's no smoking in the clubhouse or even on the golf course at Pine Valley. The back patio is the one place on the grounds where smoking is allowed. John and Mr. Smith seemed to be hitting it off so I left John alone with him to drop the hard sell.

After that, we all went upstairs and freshened up hitting the soul-cleansing showers, then met back in the dining room for dinner about forty-five minutes later. Dinner requires a jacket and tie, and if we thought lunch was good, look out. A platter of creamed spinach was served to the table—still the best I've ever had to this day. We drank Right Bank Bordeaux by the bottle, gorged ourselves on A5 Japanese wagyu filets, Maine lobster tails topped with crab bake and soufflés for dessert. We capped the meal with a high-end after-dinner port, checked the tee sheet for our tee times for the next day, and retired upstairs to our rooms. Tomorrow we would attempt to do it all again, if not for a brewing major derailment.

JAGUAR

They were lying on the grass of the clearing as evening approached. Cura spun the bracelet on Manco's wrist as he retold her the story that had been handed down in his family for eight generations of the dying jeweler, the storm, and the prophecy given to the bracelet by the priest to protect the innocent. It was peaceful until it was not. The river's hum signaled a warning. She noticed it first. The river was too loud and everything else was too quiet. There were no bird noises. The jungle had fallen silent, as if holding its collective breath in anticipation about what was about to unfold—about the blood that was about to be shed.

Cura stood up.

"Get up," she said to Manco, tugging him upright even as she spoke.

"What is it?" he asked standing now facing her with his back to the jungle's edge.

Cura's eyes darted around sensing the danger but not knowing which direction it would be coming from. She was a second too late. As the nine-foot-long brown-and-black rosette-patterned jaguar leapt upon them from the edge of the jungle she didn't have much time to react. The distance between where they were in the clearing and the jungle's edge was about two large bounds for the jaguar. As the cat left the ground, Cura shoved Manco in one direction with all of her might while she fell in the other. The jaguar missed the meat of the attack, his mighty jaws just missing the back of Manco's neck, however his long leg outstretched and his paw with four claws extended tore deep gashes into Manco's left shoulder as he cried out and fell to the ground in a spray of blood.

"Run!" he screamed.

But Cura was back on her feet and dashing for the river before the words even reached her. Manco sucked in some air and scampered to his feet as a surge of adrenaline temporarily muted the searing pain in his shoulder. However, the jaguar was on its feet just as fast and now stood between Manco and the river. The cat crouched and leapt again, not giving him time to think. Manco's instincts took over. He turned his back to the oncoming attack and simultaneously squatted into a slight crouch. As he felt the weight of the beast land on his back he employed the same over-the-shoulder throw he had used on Cura last week. Except this time there was no cuddling and kissing afterward. As soon as the cat was tossed airborne he turned and sprinted for his life toward the water. He could hear breathing and the footfall of heavy bounding steps behind him as he dove headfirst into the cool blue river water.

Up ahead, Cura had already swum to mid-river and the current was carrying her downstream. Manco swam underwater as long as he could hold his breath toward the rapid current in the middle of the river. He knew full well that jaguars were excellent swimmers and the demon had likely followed them into the water. Manco surfaced mid-river and gasped in a gulp of welcomed air. He scanned the water's surface in all directions. Cura was closer to him now. He had gained some distance. The jaguar had indeed come into the water but was swimming closer to the bank where the current was not as strong, and it was losing ground on its prey.

Cura floated as Manco swam with his good arm to

catch up to her. When he reached her they embraced.

"Are you OK!" she asked as a worried expression pained her face.

"My shoulder, it's OK," he gasped holding his left arm close to his chest.

She examined the four deep wounds. They were about twenty centimeters long tracing around the front and over the top of the shoulder. There was some skin missing and some muscle exposed, but no bone showed. The wounds were still bleeding but not pouring copious amounts of blood. His color still looked good.

"What do we do now?" he asked.

"I don't know," Cura admitted.

"Where is the jaguar?" Manco asked.

They turned back and saw that the cat had stopped and now stood in an imposing stance on the southern bank of the river staring at them.

"I guess it's giving up," said Manco.

"Or it's a lot smarter than us. Listen!" said Cura.

A growing low rumble filled their ears.

"Waterfall!" shouted Manco.

BROWN ROOM

Despite walking eighteen holes and all of the food and the booze, I couldn't sleep. I was lying in my bed. I was staring at the ceiling. I was thinking of Emily. The owl golf ball had sort of snapped me back into reality. I was taking my meds regularly and starting to think about where to go from here. I was still suspended from work. I hadn't been in contact with the hospital for nearly three weeks and I was probably fired at this point. Emily would be leaving the hospital soon and she didn't have many options left. Really her only chance was the Doxybutex. To be able to afford that we needed a bunch of money fast. The only way I could think to get that kind of cash fast was to go find the treasure. I knew where it was. I was sure of that. But I couldn't leave her at home and go get it alone. What if she died while I was gone? I needed to see her, to be with her, especially if she didn't have much time left. She would be too weak to go with me. Flying would be too difficult—out of the question with her new oxygen requirement and pulmonary embolus. I would have to decide what to do and soon.

I got out of bed and meandered down the hallway where I stumbled onto another room known as the Brown Room, which looked straight from the 1920s except for the sixty-inch flat screen that hung on the wall above the fireplace.

Oh well, I thought. If I have to throw the match again tomorrow there was no need to be well rested for that. I could do that hung over, or on no sleep, or messed up, or anything I wanted to be. The television was on the Golf Channel. I grabbed the remote and turned the volume down. I pulled my feet up under me in the high-backed soft leather lounge chair, closed my eyes and started to meditate. Or at least semi-meditate. At least clear my head. Some indeterminate amount of time went by.

I found out the service at Pine Valley is top-notch at all hours of the night because I opened my eyes a bit later and there was a bottle of scotch and a highball glass on the end table next to me. I poured myself one and took a sip. I ended up staying in that chair all night. Just thinking. Not thinking, but allowing things to come into focus. I heard once that the mind is like a jar of muddy water and thoughts become clear when we stop thinking and the sediment is allowed to settle.

By the next morning as the sun peaked over the tops of the south New Jersey pine barrens, rolled across the soft rye and poa grass of the fairways and greens of Pine Valley, slipped into the Brown Room through the wooden window slats and began to warm my cheek—I had it. *We* would go get the treasure. All three of us. I would drive. Emily could take her oxygen. Tiffany could come as well. We would get the treasure, trade it for cash and buy Emily's medicine. Nothing else mattered. That much had never been so clear to me. My scotch bottle may have been empty but my heart was full of a new hope and my resolve hardened.

We met downstairs for a breakfast bar of hot and cold items and omelets made to order in front of you by the head chef. The morning was brisk but the sun was starting to warm us as we teed off and made the first footprints of the day in the morning dew on the first fairway of the greatest golf course in the world. I noticed Mr. Smith to be a little pale and slow-moving. I figured one too many bottles of Bordeaux had taken a toll. Had I been a little more sober myself, I might have noticed the beads of sweat on his forehead—and that it was way too cool this early in the morning to sweat like that.

We took off, and the match was going well. My caddie and I were falling back into our old routine and I was lying down like a dog. After a couple of hours we had made the turn and the weather was warming up. We had shed our outer layers of golfing wind shirts and pullovers. I had grabbed a scotch on number eight when we passed by the halfway house a little earlier. We played number ten, then just off of the eleventh tee you can climb a slight embankment and get back to the halfway house should you need another snack or, in my case, another beverage. We teed off and as the caddies made their way up the fairway with the golf bags I veered right and started up the slight hill to refill my vessel with lip-smacking dark-brown nectar. I noticed Mr. Smith moving a little more slowly and his breathing was becoming more labored. I encouraged him to come up the hill with me to grab a Gatorade and he obliged.

GUNDERMAN SAYS YOU
HAVE FOUR MINUTES

We made it to the shelter and entered the small structure by the wall of logo balls. I motioned to the barkeep for a scotch and he managed to just finish my pour and replace the blue bottle on the shelf before it happened. We both felt the thud as Smith's body landed. He collapsed like a sack and then we heard the sickening crack as his skull struck the stone-tiled floor. There was a brief pause as everyone in the room took in the situation with stunned shock. We were joined just prior to the collapse by four guys playing a couple holes behind us who were just stopping in off of hole number eight. One of them knelt down and shook him, but he was not responding.

As for me, time sort of slows down in an emergency. I guess it's my training kicking in. *Four minutes,* is the first thing that always comes to mind. Back in medical school at IU we had a lecture once by an adept orator named Dr. Gunderman. I can still picture Gunderman walking up and down the steep aisles in the large lecture hall, railing on and on about *four minutes.*

"If my heart stopped right now and I collapsed," he would say, "you all would have four minutes to intervene before my brain cells started dying. You would have four minutes to act, to do something to get my blood circulating again and get oxygen delivered to my brain. And, in an emergency, with your adrenaline flowing, four minutes is an absolute eternity. You could go get a Coke from the machine in the hallway and then come back to start CPR in all likelihood," he told us. His advice when faced with an emergent situation, therefore, had always been the thing that I would fall back on and the same that I would later find reiterated in my rescue scuba diving training: STOP-BREATHE-THINK-ACT.

At this point, I modified the mantra to include my scotch: STOP-SIP-BREATHE-THINK-ACT. I took the glass off the counter and sucked down a nice pull. I then took my deep breath and was currently stuck on the THINK part of the plan. While Gunderman was right about four minutes for brain cells, I also knew that the single factor that most correlates with return of spontaneous circulation in a cardiac arrest was time to defibrillation or shock. I surveyed the room. There were some beginnings of pitiful CPR being attempted by the boys from number eight and I could tell right away that was not going to save Mr. Smith. There was no AED anywhere on the walls. I moved behind the bar and searched. None there either. STOP. Another breath. THINK—IMPROVISE—ACT.

"May I borrow your knife please?" I asked the bartender who was taking in the scene with bewildered astonishment.

He had a paring knife he had been using to quarter limes and lemons. *Good.* There was a small oscillating fan in the corner behind the bar. I leaned over, grabbed the fan, and yanked the cord from the wall. He handed me the knife. I took it and cut the electrical cord free of the fan close to the base. I then split the two wires comprising the cord with the knife and pulled them apart lengthwise for about two feet. I quickly made a circumferential cut of the plastic insulation about an inch from the end of each wire and pulled each piece off, exposing the bare wires.

"I noticed a roll of duct tape behind the bar earlier," I said to the bartender. "Toss it here please."

"Yes, sir."

"OK guys," I said, starting to direct some traffic now, "drag him over here, closer to this wall." I pointed to a wall with an outlet.

They dragged him over. I used the paring knife to cut his shirt off with a long vertical cut down the front. We peeled his cut shirt off of him and then rolled him to one side and exposed his back. He was soaked with sweat. Too much moisture. *Not good.*

"Towel!" I yelled to no one in particular. Miraculously it worked, and one was thrown in my direction by someone. I'm not sure where it came from, but I looked up and we had a good deal of spectators by now. *Might as well put them to use.*

"Someone call 911 please. Tell them we have a cardiac arrest. They can land a Medivac chopper on number seven fairway."

As I gave the instructions I used the towel to dry his back and chest as best I could with the help of someone from number eight group. I then used the duct tape to tape one of the wires to his right upper chest on the pectoral muscle above the nipple. The other one, I taped to his left lateral chest just below the nipple line. The current should be enough to kickstart the electrical activity of his heart...I hoped.

"Everybody get back! Clear! Clear! Everybody clear!" I shouted.

I surveyed the scene. No one was touching the body. I plugged the cord into the wall. Mr. Smith's body tensed so hard it seemed to jump a couple of inches off of the ground. Every lightbulb exploded and the room became darker. There was still daylight streaming in from outside though. Most striking was the sudden and overpowering stench of charred human flesh. I didn't stop long enough to think about the odor. I was on his chest immediately with good, high-quality CPR I went for a full two minutes with a ratio of thirty compressions to two breaths. I was pushing one hundred compressions per minute to the beat of "Staying Alive" by the Bee Gees, compressing the sternum at least two inches deep and allowing full recoil of the chest each time, thus giving the heart an opportunity to fill with blood between compressions.

At the two-minute/five-cycle pulse check I was covered in sweat and breathing heavily. I held compressions and moved two of my fingers to his carotid artery. *Good pulse.* I could tell by the rise and fall of his chest wall that he was breathing spontaneously now. I checked his radial pulse at the wrist. Which was good and strong as well, indicating his blood pressure was at least eighty systolic. The medics arrived a few minutes later, loading him onto a stretcher and running him to the helicopter waiting nearby on number seven fairway.

"What the hell did you do, cowboy?" one of the medics asked me as he went to start an IV and pulled away the duct tape exposing the blackened flesh underneath. The other medic winked at me.

"Hey, everybody wants to be a cowboy, but nobody wants to do cowboy shit," he said to his partner.

I ignored them both. I was suddenly very tired. I found my scotch where I had left it and downed it in one gulp. I reached over the bar, grabbed the bottle and headed out toward the shade of a large nearby pine tree. On my way out, I also grabbed the owl logo-ball and slipped it into my pocket.

BAT PHONE

My three day trip to Pine Valley was cut short by one and a half days. We changed our flights home to later that day. On the way out of the clubhouse to the shuttle Mr. Blackburn stopped me and pulled me aside over near some tiny wooden cubbies used as designated phone approved areas.

"I saw what you did, son. That was incredible. If ever there's anything the club can do for you, just say the word," he said.

He handed me a white understated business card emblazoned with the simple but iconic Pine Valley logo of a pine tree set against three different-colored vertical stripes. There were no words on either side, there was just a phone number on the back.

"Who's number?" I asked.

"Pine Valley concierge," he said with a sly smile. "Available twenty-four hours a day, three hundred and sixty-five days a year. Anything you need."

I tucked the card in my pocket, thanked him, and shook his hand. On the outside, I was calm. Inside I felt like I had just been given my own Bat phone, should I ever need a caped crusader.

PLUNGE

The deafening crash of an entire river of water falling eighty feet into a still pool below was now evident to them. They had floated all the way downstream to the falls.

"We have to swim out of this current and get to the north bank!" shouted Cura over the roar of the water.

They stroked and kicked for their lives. Cura was nearly clear of the main current when she glanced back over her shoulder. Manco was not going to make it out of the strong current swimming with one arm. The current had gained strength as they neared the falls and they were so close now they couldn't swim perpendicular to it. They had to swim somewhat against it to keep from toppling over the edge. Cura looked back at the jaguar on the southern bank, over to the northern bank now within her reach, and then to Manco behind her. Then she turned and swam back to him. He was near exhaustion. She took his left hand in hers.

"Together," she said looking him in the eyes.

She kissed him and they stopped fighting the river's destiny—the inevitability of gravity. The sheer force of the current thrust them out over the edge of the cliff about ten feet for the free fall. In the spray of the falls, as they fell downward, they held onto each other, arm-in-arm and hand-in-hand.

The force of the fall had their momentum going in slightly different directions though and they started to pull apart from each other. They tried to hold on but they could not. As Cura's hand dragged Manco's arm down and away, it caught his bracelet. The bracelet jerked free and slid off his wrist. It sparkled with a rainbow of refracted light amidst the falling water and seemed to hang in the air between them for an instant before plummeting into the water below. Manco felt his stomach drop precipitously, and it reached the water below long before the rest of his body splashed down.

GO WEST YOUNG MAN

"I'll explain it in the car. We'll have enough time together," I told her.

"I knew it! I knew you could find it!" Emily squealed.

We were loading up the Jeep with gear. Emily was already settling into the back. She was stretching out across the seat. She had it all to herself. I looked at the "essentials" she had packed: a stack of *Magical Adventure* books, Hootie the owl of course, some general maps of America, plus a few more detailed ones of the Rocky Mountain Range, including topographical maps, watersheds, and roads. She had on what she called "sporty clothes"— gym shorts, tennis shoes and a girl-power pink t-shirt. I was loading the back as she got settled. She had a small portable oxygen concentrator that delivered oxygen through the clear plastic tubing up through two prongs and into her nose, but there was no telling what kind of an adventure this could be. I still had my hospital ID badge and I had discovered that no one had bothered to deactivate it yet, so I pilfered twelve large oxygen cylinders, each about three feet tall, and I was loading them into the Jeep. Just in case.

Emily was talking a mile a minute and her excitement was palpable. Little kids' joy is so contagious. It could launch your heart and give you wings sometimes. I was excited myself. Tiffany had walked up just as I wrangled the last cylinder into the trunk. I expected an enormous suitcase packed with clothes, makeup, hairdryers and other feminine products that I wouldn't even know what to do with. Instead, to my surprise, she strode up beaming a smile with a small white carry-on-sized roller bag bearing a Whiskey Meyers sticker on the side, and a backpack. Not even a purse.

"And a good morning to you all," she greeted us.

"I expected a bigger, more girly luggage combo from you," I said.

"My dad and I used to camp before he died. I'm no princess, Dr. Beck," she teased.

I tossed her bag in the back and she got in the passenger seat. Emily was still talking to herself about endangered condors of some sort as I jumped in behind the wheel.

"OK," said Emily. "Where to? Where is it?"

"1,225 miles away. Eighteen and a half hours by car. New Mexico. The southern end of the Rockies," I said.

She let out a squeal of delight.

And we pulled out onto the road, heading for I-70, out of Indianapolis, and west.

DEFEAT

Cura surfaced first and looked around. No Manco. She scanned the river banks. No jaguar either. She waited. There was nothing else she could do. A minute went by. Bushes rustled on the southern bank of the pool. The water was still here now that she was a little way away from the falls. After what seemed like an eternity, the water's glassy surface was shattered by Manco's head as he gulped and gasped for air.

"You're OK!" exclaimed Cura.

"The bracelet! It's gone!" Manco managed to say.

"I don't care about that. I care about you," she said.

"You don't understand. It's been in my family since it was created. It was my responsibility to keep it safe. It's very special. It has special powers. It has always protected me," Manco explained, still gasping for air. "We have to find it. We have to find it now."

The bushes rustled again on the southern bank.

Cura glanced over.

"If we want to live, we have to go—now! You're hurt. The bracelet is gone. And that thing is still hunting us."

Manco knew she was right. With reluctance, a heavy heart, and a bleeding shoulder Manco followed Cura to the northern bank of the river. They lay on the rocks for a minute to gather their bearings and catch their breath, then they set out for home, defeated but alive.

Cura walked Manco as close as she could get to his home without them being seen together. She kissed him and told him she would find a way to check on him tomorrow. He stumbled into the house near dark still dripping blood from his wounded shoulder.

TO TRAP AN OCTOPUS

As we drove that first day I got know Tiffany better. It turns out I had underestimated her. This woman, while beautiful, was much more than a pretty face. She had been born in Arizona but grew up in Kansas. Her mother was a school teacher and part Native American. Her father was a driver for UPS, and he sounded like a good dad. Tiffany said they spent time on the weekends camping, hiking, and fishing. He taught her how to shoot a gun, hunt dove, and fish. She had even done some fly-fishing. She was twelve going on thirteen when her father was diagnosed with gastric cancer and twelve going on thirty when he died six short months later.

Out of necessity, she grew up overnight. She raised her younger six-year-old twin brothers, while their mother put her soul into caring for a dying husband, and then into providing for her family. The end had been quick. He tried surgery and chemotherapy but each attempt to slow the cancer growth only seemed to make him more miserable. He couldn't eat. He lost weight precipitously and his once broad-framed two hundred and thirty pounds withered to a sickly eighty-five by the time of his death. Tiffany was still jolted with pain anytime she witnessed someone vomiting after the so many nights of lying awake in their small Kansas house listening to her father groan, and wretch, and dry heave for hours on end.

"It was especially hard on Mother," she told me. "After my father died, Mother passed one week later in her sleep. Some said they were soul mates and couldn't be apart. Others said she died of a broken heart. It's silly, I know, but I've always wondered what really happened."

"Octopus trap," I blurted. Maybe I had been golfing the day they taught bedside manner in medical school.

"What did you say?" She looked at me as if I was from another planet.

"Yeah. Octopus trap. Takotsubo cardiomyopa-thy. Takotsubo is Japanese for octopus trap. There's an actual disease where if someone is in extreme stress, say they've just lost a loved one, as in your mother's case, the body produces so many endorphins and catecholamines and stress response hormones that the bottom of the heart balloons up massively while the top where the blood is supposed to flow out, con-stricts down. This ballooning effectively renders the pumping action of the heart useless. It can't do its job. It can't pump blood. Most times people just get dizzy or pass out, but for some people it can be severe enough they can die from it. I guess at one point there was a Japanese doctor who thought the imaging looked like an octopus trap. Your mother really may have died of a broken heart."

"Wow. I've never heard of that before."

"It's real. I'm sorry. That must have been a lot to go through at a young age."

"It's OK. Thanks," said Tiffany.

She looked back to see Emily dozing and snuggled up with Hootie. Her oxygen had slipped off and Tiffany reached back and curled it around each ear without waking her before carrying on with her story.

"Anyway, after both my parents died we didn't have any other family so the boys and I went into foster care. Not many families can take on three kids at once, so we got split up. It was awful. We found a foster family that could take two of us so I let the twins stay together. I was taken to a family a hundred miles away. It was rare that I got a chance to see my brothers. In the span of a year I'd lost my entire family. When I was fourteen my foster father tried to hit me. That night I packed a backpack and slipped out the window. I've been on my own ever since. I worked my way up to the paralegal job I have now. I guess it was the combination of my childhood and my current career that got me motivated to help kids like Emily. I've been guardian to five children so far, most with cancer or other terminal diseases, all with some bad luck and born into some poor social situations. None deserving of their lot in life. But none"— she hesitated as she glanced into the back seat, "quite as amazing as her."

STALE SMELL OF BEER
AND THE SMOKE IN
YOUR EYES

We rode in silence for a few miles, I suppose both of us sort of reflecting on our own lives and each other's. I flipped on the radio. Wade Bowen was singing, "Saturday Night." I decided to dig a little deeper and push my luck with Tiffany's openness.

"What about your social life?" I asked.

"All kids all the time," she said.

"What about your love life?" I ventured.

She giggled and turned up the radio but surprised

me with an answer. "I've had boyfriends but none serious. Hard to find the time. I'm paralegal by day. I spend a lot of time with guardianship duties of the children. And I'm in law school at night."

My jaw dropped a little. "I had no idea you were in law school! That's amazing. You should be proud. You've come so far, and now you are already giving back," I said.

"I am proud. And I had good years, before my parents died I mean. I'm just glad I can remember them. My brothers were young and don't remember our biological parents much. Anyway, the hard times made me into who I am today and I've been able to help a lot of people because of it. Any situation is just what you make of it," she said.

Then she smirked that smirk that made my knees weak. Her dimples showed. I thought I was going to swerve off the road. She handed me a Twizzler and our hands brushed. I managed not to crash and turned my attention back to the highway as everything new I'd just learned tumbled in my head like clumped wet clothes slapping around in the dryer.

RUN FOR THE STATE LINE

About five hours in we needed to stop for gas.

"Let's go. Get out and pee," I told Emily.

She was deep into *Ghosts in Town* and Chris and Kim were in quite a pickle.

"Just two more pages," she said.

She read aloud to us as Chris and Kim dodged swats from the ghosts close on their heels. They locked themselves in a closet as Chris fumbled with the flashlight and opened the book he had in his backpack.

"Take me there!" he screamed out loud as the ghosts approached. The next thing they knew they

169

were both awakened to a gentle breeze rustling the leaves of the trees around them back at home.

She clapped the book shut, tossed it in the seat next to her, then hopped out of the jeep and took a couple of steps.

"Forgetting something?" I asked. I grabbed her oxygen concentrator and hooked it to her waist band then looped the plastic tubing around each ear as she inserted the two small prongs, one into each nostril.

The gas station stop was remarkable only for the quantity of junk food three people could purchase. I swiped the credit card and filled up the tank. The girls went to the restroom. Then we all loaded up on snacks—bag of chips, cans of Pringles, blue slushy, red slushy, tiny candy bars, big candy bars, more Twizzlers, Tic Tacs, and some Piedmontese Beef Jerky. We all piled into the Jeep again and were back on the road in fifteen minutes.

Tiffany used her phone and found us a hotel about six hours away on the Texas-Arkansas border. I was hoping to stop sooner. I thought I could make it another six hours without a drink, but I wasn't sure. Remember that time I told you I made the three-and-a-half-hour drive to Chicago from Indianapolis in two hours flat? Well I made this six-hour run to Tex-Arkana and my cocktail in four hours and twelve minutes, and not a second too soon. I was in desperate need of a drink.

We checked into two rooms and decided we'd meet for dinner at eight o'clock at the Red Robin across the street. It was one of Emily's favorites. I rinsed off and threw on fresh jeans, a t-shirt, and cowboy boots. I splashed on some cologne and headed over early so I could be sure to get three or four drinks in before the girls got there.

I put in for a table for four, hoping to have extra room for Emily's oxygen apparatus. I never use my real name at restaurants. No particular reason. I just think it's kind of fun to make up names. This time I used "Kite," like Tom Kite the professional golfer from the eighties, who is legally blind if you can believe that. Who could imagine it? A blind golfer? And good enough to be a professional? Maybe hitting with your eyes closed is easier. I made a note to try that the next time I had a club in my hand. I pulled out a stool at the end of the bar and ordered a double Johnnie Walker Black on the rocks, two cubes, and a triple shot of chilled Codigo tequila to get started.

Ooh my. After a long day on the road, that first sip of Johnnie tasted heavenly. I swirled the glass and took a small sip. Then, deciding that the ratio of scotch to melted ice cube was acceptable, I downed half the glass on my next swig. That was followed by the chilled triple tequila shot that I didn't need the salt or lime for. A little buzz beginning, alone with my thoughts, the thing that kept playing on repeat in my head was Emily. Hard life, no fear in her though. No quit. If only everyone could share her outlook and attitude. She was remarkable. She deserved better, better than what she had been through, better than the certain and untimely death she had waiting if we didn't find that treasure.

We would need some gear. We'd have to stop at an outdoor outfitter when we got closer to the location of the treasure. We would need snack bars, bigger backpacks, a good length of rope, some climbing gear, flashlights, a tent, water bottles, and a canoe big enough to get three of us in and three of us plus the treasure out of there. I knew roughly where the old man had hidden it. I was certain of that. My real concerns were that no one else get there before us and Emily's stamina, of course. Running through every worst case scenario in my mind, if she got out there and couldn't make it back, I could possibly only carry her or the treasure back but not both. We needed both.

A tap on the shoulder from Tiffany awakened me from my daydreams. The girls had cleaned up and arrived.

"Did you get us a table?" she asked.

"Yeah. Name's in, but it's under Crenshaw," I said, still a little daydreamy.

"Crenshaw?" she asked. "Are we in incognito

- mode? Who are we hiding from?"

"No. Just a random golfer name," I answered.

About that time, "Kite party of four," was announced over the PA system. I slapped my forehead and downed the rest of my scotch.

"Ah, not Crenshaw. Blind guy. That's us. Let's go," I said.

We had a blast at dinner. Emily had been in the hospital for too long. She was so excited to be out and on an adventure. She ate the endless bowl of mac-and-cheese and refilled it three times. Orange slices on the side and a Shirley Temple to drink. We were both excited to be with her as well. After the meal we headed back across the street to the hotel. Everyone was feeling good. I dropped the girls off at their room, but I was feeling a second wind. I felt like I had fifty dollars and a flask of Crown in my pocket. Problem was I didn't have any booze in my room even, let alone in my pocket. So, I trotted around the corner to a liquor store I had noticed earlier. I found the scotch section and bought a large handle of Johnnie.

AN END TO THE DROUGHT

The next day Manco could not work. It was decided that his siblings would do his share while he rested. He choked down what little corn meal he could but he had no appetite. As he thought about it though, he couldn't tell if he was more sick from the wounds to his shoulder or from the loss of his most valuable possession.

That same morning, high-ranking nobility and priests were meeting to discuss how to end the drought. The arid weather was now a serious threat to crops across the entire land, and to the stability of the empire as a whole. The highest ruler, the *Sapa Inca*, Huayna Capac, had sent word that he wanted a swift and decisive end to the drought. It was not reflecting well on him as a ruler. Any means necessary were to be taken to ensure expedient and copious amounts of rain.

"We have given all we have to give," a top member of the nobility stated.

"Every Incan sacrifices what they can to Illapa and prays daily," another confirmed.

"We could double our prayers," suggested one of the common priests.

"Illapa is not listening. The finest five of our black-woolen llamas were tied up for a week with no water and Illapa refused to hear their cries of thirst. They have since died on the rope."

"Then we only have one course of action left," said another nobleman. "We must appeal to Illapa's kind heart with a greater sacrifice."

Silence washed over the room.

"A fine daughter of noble blood then," suggested a priest when someone finally spoke again.

There were many noblemen of royal blood in the room and while it was an honor to sacrifice your child's life to a god, it was still your child. More silence followed.

It was the high priest who finally broke it.

"We need not get carried away. The *Sapa Inca* has asked for results but demanded nothing specific. Let us not spill noble blood at this point if we don't have to. Dispatch troops to the orphanage and select a suitable human sacrifice. We will start our sacrifices with one of those children."

STORMS

There weren't supposed to be storms. That's all I could think. But the thunder. The thunder would not cease. *Boom. Boom. Boom!* And with every bolt of lightning and rumble of thunder, I felt a jolt of pain in the left side of my head almost as if the storm were on top of me or inside me and the lightning was striking me in my left eye. I had no sense of time or space. No idea of what time it was or where I was, yet the thunder continued. Pauses, then grouped repetitive bursts. *BOOM! BOOM! BOOM!* in rapid succession.

I reached up and clutched my head, noticing

a pillow. I pulled it tight around my head. *I must be in a bed,* I thought and buried myself deeper under the covers. The pounding continued and my senses started to return. As they did, I realized it wasn't a storm. Someone was beating on my hotel room door. I mustered some strength and slid off the bed to the floor with a thump. A completely empty handle of scotch clattered down to the floor with me as well.

Oh shit, I thought, as a few memories began to return from last night. I crawled to the door, pulled myself up a little, flipped the lock, and cracked it open. Tiffany stopped banging on the door. She and Emily stepped over me into the room.

"My God, we've been knocking for ten minutes. We thought you were dead," she exclaimed. "Are you OK?"

She glanced around the room and at that point noticed the enormous empty handle of scotch. She didn't say a word. I peered up at her from my position still on the floor. I must have looked like hell judging by the expression on her face. I didn't say anything, just stood up, sidestepped her, and tried to make it to the bathroom. I didn't make it in time. I began vomiting in the trash can under the desk. Tiffany took Emily by the hand and led her out of the room without looking back.

Toward the late afternoon, still in bed but with my headache dying down, Tiffany reentered. She was alone this time.

"I brought you some soup," she said as she placed a Styrofoam cup on the nightstand bedside the bed. I moved my feet and she sat down on the foot of the bed.

"Thanks," I said after a pause.

Tiffany started to speak again then stopped. She looked away before she spoke again. "We're doing this for her. We're doing this for Emily. How could you be so selfish?"

I was silent.

She stared at the floor for a long time before beginning again.

"We're at a crossroads. And it's up to you at this point. We can't do this without you. And we can't do it with you drunk or hung over and nonfunctional every day. You have to choose between your addiction and her life. And her time is running out. There is no more time. You have to choose now. And right now, you're already making your choice whether you realize it or not."

Tears rolled over the arch of her perfect cheekbones and spilled down to the bedsheet.

"I don't quit on people, Tom. I'm not giving up on Emily. But I will give up on you if you force me to choose. Don't put me in that position. Please?" She stood and walked out, closing the door softly behind her.

AN EXCHANGE FOR RAIN

Manco was lying in his bed sweating in the hot still air when the troops arrived. All the other kids were in the fields. He was thankful for that. His mother had mended his wounds, but she did not fight against the soldiers. What could she do? She pleaded with them but her words fell on deaf ears. She hugged Manco.

"It's OK," he told her, forcing himself to smile.

Then he went along calmly. Hidden from view, Cura watched the scene from a nearby hillside. Pleas to her father had no place. Decisions had been made, and to beg for the life of an orphan boy would expose their affair.

Word was sent out across the empire that tomorrow at noon, on an altar of the great temple, there would be a human sacrifice to Illapa in exchange for rain.

WISH THAT MY ADDICTIONS DIDN'T MEAN SO MUCH

The next morning I knew what I had to do. And I was ready to face the truth of the matter—this was going to hurt. The decision wasn't hard. It just took some mental pep talks to prepare myself for the pain. Unlike opioid withdrawal which is just plain awful itself, alcohol withdrawal can kill you. There are the sweats, jitteriness, shakes, and diarrhea, but depending on how accustomed your body was to having alcohol in it, it could also progress to tachycardia, fever, confusion, hallucinations, seizures, and death. Under normal circumstances, the process is monitored in a hospital with IV medications and vital sign monitoring under a doctor's care. I had a hotel room on the Texas-Arkansas border, a pretty paralegal, and a dying nine-year-old.

Going to a hospital was out of the question. It would take too much time. Plus, there is a huge bias and stigma against doctors with substance abuse problems. Public knowledge of this would ruin my career. And right now it was going oh-so-swimmingly.[1]

No. This was the only way, and like I said, it was gonna hurt. I had a script pad in the Jeep and wrote a prescription for some Valium under Tiffany's name which she went to go fill at a pharmacy in town. I was able to write for a bag of IV fluids and a butterfly needle under Emily's name. I also had Tiffany go to a hardware store and pick up four three-foot-long pieces of twine. While she was gone I explained to Emily that we were extending our stop here for a little bit, and that I would be...eh...not myself for about three days to say the least. I promised, though, that when I came out the other side, I would be better than ever.

---

[1] For further reading on the stigma against physicians with mental health or addiction problems an excellent read is, *A Long Walk Out of the Woods* by Adam Hill

Tiffany returned and I went over the instructions with her in detail. After about a day without alcohol in my system, my body would start to react. At that point, I would start experiencing the withdrawal symptoms and need to start taking the Valium. I would become sedated and confused, and Tiffany would need to keep feeding me the Valium pills every few hours, or possibly even more frequently, to prevent seizures. I warned her that I wouldn't be myself and things would get ugly. At some point I would become unable to eat and drink. That was when she would need to use the twine to tie my wrists and ankles to the bed to keep me from hurting myself or someone else. The butterfly needle could then be placed between the skin and the muscle tissue, and the fluids could be given via a slow infusion up to thirty milliliters per hour in a process called hypodermoclysis. That should give me enough fluid to sustain my hydration while unable to eat and drink. It would be easier to manage than an IV for an untrained person, and we didn't have any IV supplies anyway.

I anticipated the process would take three days, but that was a best-case scenario. What I wasn't telling the girls was that in severe cases I had seen it take seven or eight days. But that was time we didn't have. I showed Tiffany how to tie the twine in knots that I wouldn't be able to get out of, and showed her how to insert the needle under the skin but still keep it lying on top of the muscle not down into it. We didn't have much time before I was sure to start feeling bad. I hadn't drank since the night before last, so I gave Emily her enoxaparin injection under the skin of her abdomen for the evening then read her a *Magical Adventure* book about Chris and Kim called *Lions out to Lunch*.

Chris and Kim managed to miss being lunch on the African plains to some hungry lions, and made it back just in time to say the magic phrase.

"Take me there," said Emily for them as she closed her eyes and drifted off to sleep as we finished.

I pulled the covers up and kissed her forehead. I then went next door to my own room. I had lions of my own to fight. I looked in the mirror at a sweat-beaded forehead, saw fear and doubt in my eyes and took my first of many Valium with an already trembling hand.

SLEEPLESS

That night was sleepless for many across the empire. The *Sapa Inca*, Huayna Capac, lay awake worrying about the fate of his empire should rain not come, the crops die, and his people begin to starve and revolt. The high priest stood erect beside a bright-burning fire and prayed through the entire night. A large jaguar stalked the riverbanks, angry, hungry, listless, and determined to catch that which had evaded it yesterday.

Manco lay awake in an Incan prison shackled to the wall and dreaming of all the future times he would not get to share with his lover, Cura. Cura lay awake, staring at the glittering stars in the galaxy, counting frequent falling stars this evening, refusing to complacently accept this dealt hand, and contemplating how she could change it. But what could she do? She was only a girl in a world run by men. And decisions had been made. And her noble blood line had no sway in the matter it seemed.

KINK

I awoke to darkness. The first thing I noticed was pain in my wrists. I wasn't tied up anymore, but both wrists had circumferential rope burns around them. They were bleeding, but not a lot. I stirred and rubbed my wrists.

"Ugh," I groaned.

Tiffany was sleeping in the chair in the corner of the room and she awakened to my moaning.

"Welcome back," she whispered.

"How long has it been?" I managed to ask, pulling myself up to a sitting position on the side of the bed.

"Four days," she answered.

"Shit. Any issues?" I asked.

She paused. "The hallucinations were pretty bad at one point. You were carrying on about the treasure and getting there before anyone else. I'm glad you came back to us when you did. We are out of Valium.

"There was an episode as well that took some quick thinking on my part," she paused again. "Maybe it's best to not tell you about it."

"We're friends," I coaxed.

"OK. At first I forgot to put the 'Do Not Disturb' sign on the door and the housekeeper came in and found you tied to the bed in four-point restraints. I thought she was going to call the police."

"What did you do?" I asked.

"I just straddled and crawled on top of you, licked your cheek, and told her this is how we liked it," she laughed.

"Kinky. Nice job. Which cheek? I'll never wash it," I joked.

"Wouldn't you like to know?"

"Emily's OK?" I asked.

"She's OK. She's bored. She's read every *Magical Adventure* book we brought. Three times. But she's OK. We need to get back on the road. When do you think you'll be up to it?"

I made sure my arms and legs were functional,

and stood up carefully. I was weak and I suddenly noticed a painful hunger in my churning stomach.

"Let me get some food and I'll go over the plans with you guys tonight. We can hit the road again in the morning. Is Emily asleep?" I asked.

"We'll wake her. She'll want to see you. Come on, let's find you some food," Tiffany said.

We were able to order in some Thai food. I ate and ate and ate. We had to place a second order when I finished off all of the pad thai, tom-yum soup, and spring rolls.

Emily was overjoyed to see me, and I likewise her. We shared a long hug at the sight of each other and experienced one of those rare moments in life when no words were necessary and both parties recognized it. As we ate, I explained my solve of the riddle and where we would find the treasure.

SOLVE

I talked as I ate. "Here's the poem again." I started to write it down, but Emily had it memorized and recited it as I wrote:

> "The truth̲s of the treasure
> Come to One who is bold
> Who is called down under
> WeT and cold
> ApprOach the souRce
> Through the flow of the flood
> To stay afloat

To stay above
Then come upon
The sOund made like thunder
Where paths are crossed
As the Meek shall waNder
The mark below
The eyes of the owl
Under the call
Of the biG cat's wail
Seek the treasure
Laid quickly down in the wOod
When all is answered
As dreams only could"

"Most people are thrown off right from the start," I began. "We'll start with the first line, then ignore the rest of that first stanza for now. We'll come back to it later. People are scattered all over the Rockies looking for the correct body of flowing water at which to start their search. But, to understand this poem and the hidden meanings behind it, you have to start in the right place. And to start in the right place you have to understand the man who wrote the poem. Donovan's later life centered around Native American culture. That is the fundamental knowledge block needed to stand on to solve the poem."

"So where does it tell us to start?" Tiffany asked.

"Right. First, we need to remember what Mr. Dean said in some of his interviews about the treasure. I've watched them all many times over, and a couple of times he slipped up and gave away some details that I don't think he intended. In one particular interview he said he left home that morning to hide the treasure and came back to sleep in his own bed that night. He lives in Santa Fe, so we have to be dealing with the southern end of the Rocky Mountain chain."

Emily was smiling at me and Tiffany was frowning.

"That's still an enormous area and no certain starting point," Tiffany said.

"Tell her! Tell her!" Emily was all but jumping up and down.

"I did share this one detail with Emily earlier. You can tell her the definition, Em."

Emily's eyes brightened.

"Tao. The way. The path. The right way. The Truth," she quoted.

"Also," I added, "That, in virtue, of which all things happen or exist. The definition of 'Tao.' It took extensive digging, but I found it. The word 'truth<u>s</u>' in the first line gives us the starting point. Truth is the only word that is needed there. The 's' is unnatural and it must have more significance."

"And so if you add the underlined 's' from the poem 'Tao' becomes Taos, New Mexico," said Emily.

"We have a jumping-off point," I confirmed.

"That's the hardest part. The rest sort of falls into place from there. Where do we go when we get to Taos? What does the poem say? 'Approach the source through the flow of the flood.' Emily you have a detailed map of Taos and the surrounding area?" I asked.

"Right!" she replied, her excitement growing as she began rustling through her backpack for the correct map. When she had it, she spread it out across the floor and we all hunkered over it.

"OK. Here's the city of Taos," she said.

"Flow of the flood. Are we looking for a river?" asked Tiffany.

"Yes. Let's see what major waterways are in the area."

"There's the Rio Grande. That's massive," said Emily. "Here's another one. It looks like the only other river in the area, the Rio Pueblo de Taos."

"Let's assume that's the one for now," I said.

"But how do we know where to get on the river and where to get off?" asked Tiffany.

"I don't think it matters where we get on as long as we get off at the right spot. Let's keep going with the clues and you'll see," I answered.

"OK, what's the next line?" Tiffany was getting excited now as well. She had heard snippets of this before in the ramen restaurant after my manic break but I hadn't gone into this kind of detail with her at the time.

"Then come upon
The sOund made like thunder"

"Sound made like thunder? What in the world does that mean?" Tiffany asked.

"It means we put our canoe in the Pueblo River in the Taos Canyon," I said. "And we follow it until we hear a thunderous sound."

"What would make a thunderous sound?" asked Emily.

"Let's check the map," I suggested.

She ran her finger along the length of the river. Where the Pueblo River met the Rio Grande there was a notation on the map signifying whitewater rapids. She double tapped the map and smiled.

"I wonder if you can hear a roar from the rapids." She said. "Here it's marked Sunset Rapids."

"They must be pretty significant rapids if they've earned their own name and a notation on a map," I suggested.

"So, we hit the river and as soon as we hear the roar of the rapids, we make our next move," I continued.

"And what would be our next move?" Tiffany asked.

"We need a short history lesson to understand the next two lines. They are:

Where paths are crossed
As the Meek shall waNder

"In the spring of 1845 Independence, Missouri, was buzzing with settlers preparing their wagon trains to head west hoping to settle in California and Oregon. Some were heading out seeking free government land, others were taking part in the gold rush. The ones who were bound for Oregon would end up on the famous wagon route we know as the Oregon Trail. You guys know who one of the most famous guides on that trail was?" I asked them.

Both shook their heads no so I continued.

"Stephen Meek. It's interesting, though, he's not famous for his great successes in leading thousands of wagons west. He's famous for a disastrous shortcut he tried to take a couple hundred wagons on in 1845. Instead of sticking with the original Oregon Trail route and going up above the Columbia River to the headwaters of the Willamette Valley, he convinced his wagon train to follow him on a shortcut across the east Oregon desert. It's known now as Meek's Cutoff. They got lost out there and ran out of water. They were lost for months. About thirty of the settlers died before eventually making it to their destination. It was a colossal failure.

"Here's where it ties into our poem: By the time they were found by some Native Americans and got help figuring out where they were, the settlers had had enough of Meek's guidance. They had just made it to the Deschutes River and had to find a way to cross it. As their cattle were fording across, word came from the back of the train that some of the settlers were on their way forward to kill Meek and his wife. This forced Meek and his wife to hastily abandon the rest of the party and cross the river to the northwest side.

"'As the Meek shall waNder,' is a message to do as Meek did in 1845 and cross to the northern bank of the river. The southeastern bank of the river with the mutinous pioneers meant certain death for Meek and his wife, so the northern bank of our river is where we go."

"Unbelievable," Tiffany said. She then pondered a bit. "But wait a minute, Meek is capitalized because it's a proper noun, but there are lots of other random letters capitalized in the poem. What do they mean?"

"About that...I honestly don't know," I responded with a twisted face. "They don't seem to spell anything that I can decipher. But on a side note, it is documented that Meek was in Taos in the spring of 1838," I added for the random historical reference.

"OK, history class is over. Next stanza:

The mark below
The eyes of the owl
Under the call
Of the biG cat's wail.

"This is where we look for some symbol of significance. Could be anything really. Rocks stacked to
look like an owl face. A carving in a tree. We'll find the
marking when we get on site. Will you please read the
next stanza, Emily?" I asked.

"Seek the treasure
Laid quickly down in the wOod
When all is answered
As dreams only could"

Tiffany sat back a little stunned soaking it all in.

"What about the first paragraph that we ignored at
the start of this thing?" she asked when she snapped
back to us.

"Perfect timing. This is when we need to come
back to that first paragraph.

The truths of the treasure
Come to One who is bold

Who is called down under
WeT and cold

"Most Native American cultures believed life to be circular, not linear. So you read the poem in a circle, not the strictly left-to-right, top-to-bottom way that we normally read. We began in the second stanza, and now we circle back to the first, which I believe indicates the treasure may ultimately be in a wet, wooded area. The references to wet and cold suggest it may even be submerged," I concluded, wrapping up my case.

Emily gave me a hug. We decided to set out early the next morning. We thought we should be able to reach Taos and get our gear sorted by the next evening. As I put Emily into bed that night she pinched the scant amount of belly fat she could find, and I stuck the needle under the skin giving her the blood thinner injection. We took a journey of the imagination through a book to the time of the dinosaurs where we helped Chris and Kim explore and eventually escape home as Emily drifted off to sleep, no doubt dreaming of adventures of her own.

LEAP

Cura snuck through the jungle as the first morning light was just streaking through the green canopy of tree tops. She slowed her pace to a crawl as she neared the river and the jaguar's territory, careful to not make even a squeak of noise. Cura would decide her own fate. No man would script it for her. She reached the river's edge. It rolled along as if in conversation with the calm morning air. She crouched down and stayed completely still for twenty minutes until she was sure the jaguar was not lying in wait. When she was confident that the sounds of the jungle were normal and unworried, she advanced to the edge of the water and followed it downstream until she at last reached the waterfall. She peered over the edge of the cliff.

How did we survive that fall, she wondered? Getting down there safely again was going to be another problem. There were sheer rocky cliff faces on either side of the falls. Scaling either of them would be slow and dangerous. Going around through the jungle was even less appealing, especially with the jaguar still out there hunting her. She could jump in the river and tumble over the falls again but that didn't seem smart either.

She studied the area. About ten feet from the cliff's edge was a tall tree. She eyed it up and down. If she could make the leap to the tree and hang on she could shimmy down it to the safety of the ground. It seemed to be the safest route at this point—if she could make the jump. Her fate, she told herself. She eyed a spot on the tree for each hand to grab onto when she landed. She got a running start, reached the edge of the cliff, threw her arms in the air, her head back, and leapt like she had wings.

INSTINCT - BASED
MEDICINE

We hit the road early the next morning. We had all slept well and were more than excited to move on from this place. A few hours in we stopped for gas and Emily wanted to learn how to pump it. I brought her over and taught her to swipe the card. She undid the gas cap, and selected the proper grade of fuel. We were standing there while the tank filled, enjoying the morning sun on our faces and the sounds drifting over from the nearby highway, when blood sprang from her nose like a fountain. It poured out and down her face, onto her hand and the gas pump handle. She noticed it first and screamed from shock. My hand shot out and I pinched just below the bridge of her nose.

"It's OK. Tilt your head back. It's OK," I comforted her.

She was surprised but not scared. I looked around. Tiffany was inside using the restroom.

"OK. Hold your nose here where I'm holding it and sit on the running board of the car," I said as I handed her nose back to her. I opened the back door of the Jeep and sat her down then went to grab a handful of paper towels from the dispenser below the window squeegee.

I started cleaning her up as best I could. Emily was settling down, but there was blood everywhere.

Tiffany came out right about then.

"My God. What's happened!" she cried.

"Just a bloody nose. We'll get her cleaned up. It will be OK. Can you take her in to the restroom to wash up please?" I asked.

"Of course. Come on, dear." Tiffany led her inside by one hand. Emily still pinched her nose with the other.

I stood by the Jeep and worried a bit to myself. A common side effect of the continuous oxygen is that it can dry out your nose and leave the thin lining of the nasal passages prone to bleeding, but this was a gusher. She was on the blood thinning shots to keep her blood from clotting and that was not something that could be stopped.

Still, I'd always been a proponent of what I call, "instinct-based medicine"— and my instincts were making me uneasy.

DIVE

Cura was a couple hours into the day by this point and didn't have much more time. Manco was to be sacrificed when the sun was highest in the sky. Manco seemed to believe in the bracelet's value. Cura hoped the priest would think it was valuable, too. She was hoping to trade it for Manco's life. She undressed and laid her clothes on the bank near the pool of water at the base of the waterfall.

You can do this, she told herself.

Not knowing how deep the bottom was, she filled her lungs full of air, dove in and down. The chill of the cool water washed over her body. She swam down and down, deeper and deeper, her arm outstretched and reaching for the bottom. The pressure built in her ears and still she swam down, but still no bottom found her hand. Her lungs burned as she turned and kicked up to the surface where she gulped delicious air. Once she had caught her breath she steeled her resolve.

On her next attempt she realized it was using up too much of her energy to kick down to the bottom while fighting two buoyant lungs full of air. She went to the shore and found the heaviest rock she could lift. She took deep and rapid breaths until she was almost dizzy, then she let the rock pull her down. They sank together, conserving her oxygen and her strength. She landed with a soft thud on the bottom and began to feel around blindly with her hand in a circular pattern. It was deep and dark. She opened her eyes but couldn't see anything.

To her delight, though, it was not a muddy bottom, it was rocky. The bracelet would be hard to find but at least it wouldn't be sunk down and buried in soft mud. The morning continued in that pattern. She would crash to the bottom, about twenty feet deep, and search in the darkness with her hands until her lungs burned like they were full of fire. Then she would bolt to the surface, gather her breath, find another big rock, and repeat.

RELATIVITY

I still find it odd but decidedly true how time is relative. Einstein proved it with an equation. It seems to travel more slowly when you're bored and to fly by when you're engaged in activity or things are going your way. I'm not exactly sure that's what Einstein's equation even proves, but I do know things for us happened quickly indeed after that nosebleed— to the point of becoming a blur. Camus described it once as time taking on its most extreme dimensions. All three of us had gold fever. We could feel gold in our hands, imagine it running through our fingers, and feel the weight of it filling our pockets. We checked into the self-proclaimed Historic Taos Inn. The Inn had been operating since 1936 and seemed quaint and comfortable. Tiffany and I chose it because you can enter the rooms from the outside. You don't have to enter through a central lobby to reach each guestroom. And it had a pool. Maybe Emily could take her oxygen off and swim a little. Much to my chagrin, the website, as well as the billboard out front, boasted about their award-winning margaritas. Boy, did I pick a bad time to sober up.

It was late in the day when we arrived. The rooms were nice and clean and each one had a wood burning fireplace in the corner to help you fend off the cold desert nights. We checked in and I took Emily to the pool for a swim. She would take her oxygen off and get in the water, swim around for about four or five arm strokes until her hunger for air overwhelmed her, then pull herself to the side, breathe the oxygen for a couple minutes, and repeat.

Back in the room we lit a fire. Tiffany had gotten us some tacos and we ate while I read to everyone from one of Emily's books.

When I went to tuck Emily in, she was squeezing her eyes closed. I had yet to give her the evening injection though, and she was not a good enough actress to convince me she was actually asleep.

"Hey, you're not liking these shots, huh?" I asked.

"Not one bit," she said.

"I have an idea. Let's try this: Close your eyes and go somewhere else when things are getting bad. Just like Chris and Kim do in the books. Give it a try. Where do you want to go?" I asked.

"OK. I'll try to go to a beach. I've never been to one before." She closed her eyes again and whispered, "Take me there."

"Imagine that," I whispered back, "the warm sun is on your face and the waves are lapping up on the beach one after the other."

I gave her some time and did not say anything else. Her body had relaxed. The tension was gone.

"I feel good now. You can give me the shot," she said.

I laughed. "I gave it to you a couple minutes ago, kid. Good night."

The next morning, the rain god spoke as if announcing our arrival. I'm unsure if he was voicing his approval or disapproval. It was like nothing I've ever seen before. The locals stared up in awe. The water ran in small rivers in the streets. The skies opened up and dumped monsoon-caliber rain on the city of Taos. Walls of rain pounded the hotel in ceaseless waves. We were able to grab some local fruit at one of the nearby stores without drowning, but we were holed up for the day for sure. Emily swam in the indoor hotel pool. Lightning streaked the sky and thunder rumbled throughout the day. It was a spectacular show with the mountains in the background. We sat near the window and took it all in. We cracked it a bit to let the wet smell of the rain in.

The rhythms of the rain were soothing. In our small bubble with each other, we felt protected from the chaos of the storm, even as everything else around us was ravaged. We were close to the treasure and we could feel it. The treasure wanted to be found, but it would have to wait one more day for us. We lounged, snacked on fruit, read, joked with each other, watched nature unleash her fury, experienced just being with each other, and did a lot of nothing. And it's one of the fondest days in my memory. I have always been grateful for that storm and the extra day it gave us.

A GOOD LENGTH
OF ROPE

Taos Mountain Outfitters had all the gear I thought we would need to grab this box of loot. And they had a dog as well. It seemed to have mange. It was at least mangy looking. Emily loved it immediately.

"Oh God. Don't touch it," I said.

"He likes being petted. And Hootie likes him, too," she said as she nestled her owl in tight next to the scraggly beast.

I had forgotten to give Emily her morning shot so I took care of it while she was petting the dog by the front door. Someone walked in behind us as I finished up, but I didn't turn to see who it was.

A short while later, Tiffany and I were buying the last of our gear and talking to the salesman near the back of the store. His name tag read: Gary Butts. There weren't many other shoppers in there yet. It was morning and they had just opened. We were stocking up on flashlights, backpacks, and a good length of rope. I had no idea why we would need a good length of rope. I just felt if you were going on an outdoor adventure it was a "must have." Bear Grylls probably doesn't get up at night to take a piss at home without a good length of rope slung over one shoulder, and I certainly wasn't going into the desert on a treasure hunt without one. Anyway, we were both wrapped up in picking out a canoe to rent. I realized I didn't hear Emily's voice talking to the dog anymore so I called her name.

No answer came back.

I walked around the corner so I could see where she had been sitting with the dog, but she wasn't there. I left Tiffany at the counter with Gary and walked up to the front of the store. The mange dog was there and Hootie was wedged under his leg. Something was wrong. She wouldn't leave the owl. I shot back to the counter.

"Emily's missing. Tiffany, check the street by where we came in. Gary, you have surveillance cameras in here?" I asked the clerk, pointing to one up in the corner behind the counter.

"No, they're just decoys to scare shoplifters," he said, reeling backward. "I can call the Taos PD for you."

"Hold on that right now, Buttsie. Is there another exit to this place?" I asked.

"Sure. Out back and through the storage area." He pointed to a door at the back of the store.

"OK, you search the rest of the store and I'll head out the back," I ordered.

I went through a door at the back of the shop and into the warehouse. No sign of the girl. There was a door on the back wall that I was sure would lead to an alley behind the shop. I was headed that way when I noticed one of Emily's maps from her pack on the floor. She must have dropped it there. It was next to the door to a small utility closet. I crept close to the door. I heard voices inside, so I leaned my ear against the door.

"Give me the drugs, kid," a gruff voice commanded.

"I don't have drugs you creep," I heard Emily reply.

"I know you have them. I saw you with needles. You don't want to get hurt."

It must be the guy who walked in while I was finishing giving Emily her shot by the door, I thought. *He must have seen me put the needles and vials of medication into Emily's backpack, and thought she had opioids in there. OK, that was about enough of that.*

KEVIN KISNER

PGA tour great, Kevin Kisner, has always been excellent at the golf format called match play. That's one golfer versus another in a one-on-one match where each hole is worth one point. He was once quoted in an interview as saying the best part about match play is that "you get to beat someone's ass." Well, if there's ever been anything positive to come out of a drug addict threating someone you love, I guess I just think of Kisner and how I "get to beat someone's ass."

The door opened inward and I slammed into it as hard as I could. Our druggie perpetrator was just inside and it hit him hard. Emily was crouching behind her backpack in the back corner of the small closet-sized room. The force of the door pushed the bad guy into the wall but he had reached into the small of his back and was pulling out a large knife. He was pinned behind the door though and couldn't maneuver well. I grabbed the wrist holding the knife with my left hand and pushed it against the wall. Then I broke his nose with a right cross. He reached for his bleeding nose and I grabbed a paint can off the shelf nearby and dented it over his head. He collapsed to the ground with a thud.

I went to Emily and checked to see that she was okay. I looked her over and hugged her close to me. She seemed to be fine.

I moved back to the downed man. He was unconscious but breathing. His nose was bleeding and a goose egg was growing on his head. I stuck a finger in each of his ears. No blood or clear spinal fluid was coming from them which could have indicated a basilar skull fracture. *All good things.*

Still, "hillbilly out for broken nose revenge," was one thing I didn't want to deal with. If he had seen Emily's maps he might even know our planned route or have an idea of our destination. I looked around the room but there wasn't anything handy with which to tie him up. I didn't want the police involved with this either for a lot of reasons. When I rolled him over onto his back, I noticed a skinny piece of clear tubing running from a small battery-pack-looking box on his belt to an insertion site on his abdominal wall.

Well, chemical restraint can be just as good as physical, I thought. He's a diabetic. An insulin-dependent type 1 diabetic with an insulin pump to be precise. The little box on his belt was delivering insulin at a continuous rate through the tubing to the insertion site under his skin. I smirked a little. This would be creative even by my standards. We could take the pump off of him and send his body into diabetic ketoacidosis. He would get uncontrollable nausea and vomiting. His blood pH would plummet as acid built up in his system. His electrolytes would get very much out of whack and he would be rendered nonfunctional for a couple days. But, it could take hours or possibly days for all that to set in. We didn't have that kind of time. We needed him to stay here and quiet, at least for the next few hours. However, if I reprogrammed his pump to give him a lot more insulin than normal, but not so much as to kill him, then he would take a long hypoglycemic nap. It was pretty dangerous, but also fast-acting. I unclipped the pump from his belt and made the adjustments to the settings based on my estimate of his body weight. *There we go.* I re-clipped the pump to his belt. I took

Emily by the hand, flipped off the light, and we closed the door. I told Emily we should keep this to ourselves. Back at the counter, we paid Gary and split.

"I found her out in the back alley wandering off. You know kids. We'll give her a talking to," I told the store clerk. Tiffany and Emily started hauling gear out and Gary helped me load the canoe onto the roof of the Jeep. We strapped it down and the three of us were each one step closer to our fate.

SEE IT IN YOUR MIND

Manco sat awake and waiting for the guards that morning, anticipating the long walk up the mountainside to the temple. He did not resist. He was not resigned to his fate. He still held out hope, but fighting or fleeing at this point was not an option. He began the arduous, escorted walk toward his fate as Cura continued to dive. They walked throughout the morning. He reached the foot of the temple about an hour and a half before Inti would peak in the sky—and his life was scripted to end.

The ceremony was already underway. Fires

blazed as songs were sung, chants were chanted, and prayers were prayed. An enormous crowd of over two hundred thousand Incans had gathered. The air hung thick, heavy, and sticky on everyone with anticipation.

At the exact moment Manco looked up at the sun to judge the time, Cura was doing the same while treading water.

It has to be here, she told herself. She had to find it. She closed her eyes and re-envisioned toppling over the waterfall two days prior. In her mind, she saw the bracelet slide off of Manco's wrist and hang in mid-air. She saw it fall amidst the cascade of water. She saw where it landed in the water, especially where it fell in relation to the splashes of the crashing water striking the still pool. She did not return to shore for another rock. She sucked in a breath, dove and kicked down with vigor. She searched the spot where she'd seen it land in her mind. She felt around on the bottom until her lungs screamed for air. She felt fire in her throat. It was all she could do to keep her body from breathing in lungs full of water. Right when she realized she couldn't stay down any longer, her hand brushed something metallic. She touched it again. It was round and hoop shaped. She grasped it and bolted toward the surface. She was oxygen deprived, and when she first emerged she opened her eyes but she still could not see. A few moments later oxygenated blood flow was returning to her brain and her vision came into focus. The object in her right hand glinted in the light. It was Manco's bracelet.

DANGER MERIDIAN

Now, looking back, I wonder why. Why at this point we didn't stop and evaluate our risk to return on investment? Back when John-Boy and I were growing up and doing stupid shit, at certain points along the course of each tragedy we would stop and assess ourselves, our risk, and our situation. Once we crossed a point where the risk to anyone involved in completing the task at hand had gone up exponentially, and our perceived chance of success had gone down proportionally, we said that we had crossed a line on a graph. This principle is known as crossing a danger meridian.

John and I didn't have such a fancy name for it back in our day, but we were calculating the same thing in our heads. When you cross that line, at that point your mission, the course that you are on poses more risk to all of you than potential gain.

In the future.

In retrospect.

Looking back.

This was that point for the three of us on this treasure hunt, even if we didn't realize it at the time.

THE FLOW OF THE FLOOD

Highway 110 leads you out of the great city of Taos and straight to the lower Taos River where we parked, unloaded our gear, and launched our canoe into the river. Everyone was fitted with a lifejacket. Tiffany tightened Emily's snug.

"Tom," she said, "come take a look at Emily's oxygen concentrator. It seems to be hissing.

I walked over and examined the unit and found it to be cracked and leaking. Definitely not working like it should. It must have broken during the scuffle in the outfitters shop. There was no fixing it. Not out here for sure.

"Well, we can use the big tanks. Less ideal to haul around out here, but at least you can still go kid," I told her.

I replaced the oxygen concentrator on her hip with one of the large tanks on a two-wheeled cart. I didn't know for sure what we might run into so I threw six extra oxygen tanks into the canoe and tied them down. Emily stared at the cascading water. The river was raging and full of roiling water. The spring ice melt had come down from the mountains and along with yesterday's rains it was flowing in a torrent.

YOU'RE NOT YOURSELF
WITHOUT A SNICKERS

With the canoe half in the water, I made sure the girls were in and went back to the Jeep one last time. I had to make a call. I had been over it in my mind several times and I decided I might be a dick at times, but I was not a murderer. I blocked my cell phone number and called the outfitter shop.

"Hello. Taos Mountain Outfitters. This is Gary," the answer came.

"Gary, there's an unconscious man in the utility closet of your back room. When you go to wake him remove his belt and the pump on it as well. And take him two Snickers bars and a Coke."

I ended the call, turned off the phone, chucked it onto the driver's seat, and headed for the canoe, the river, and glory.

NO TIME

Cura swam to shore and dressed. She again looked up at the sun ambling across the sky. There was no time left.

Manco walked up the imposing steps of the temple toward the clouds and the sacrificial stone. Cura was fifteen miles away and Manco had about one hour of his life left.

She ran.

She ran through the jungle. There was crashing in the brush behind her. She didn't look back. She ran harder. Her focus narrowed. The world faded away and she melted into herself. She emerged from the jungle and made it to the road system. Every time she hurt she ran harder. She used her pain as fuel. The more her feet hurt, the harder she ran. As her muscles ached, she pushed harder. As her lungs burned, she imagined herself on fire—a ball of flames unstoppable on its quest. She pushed on. Today she would write her own story. She was smart. She was strong. She was woman.

TO STAY AFLOAT
TO STAY ABOVE

The boat ride was a treasure itself. The weather was sterling, and the desert scenery exuded peace and calm. The sun glinted off the high rock banks flanking the river, reflected off the water, and Tiffany's light brown skin glowed in it. Emily sat at the front of the boat and trailed her hands in the water. I wish it could have just gone on like that forever.

A couple of hours passed in the blink of an eye. I could see up ahead, maybe five-hundred yards away, the merging of our Pueblo de Taos River with the raging Rio Grande. Emily heard it first and I saw her head pop up to attention, a low rumble you could almost feel before you heard it. A few yards farther on we all heard the thunder-like rumble from Sunset Rapids on the Grande.

"That's got to be the rapids," she said. "The sound like thunder."

"I think this is the spot," I announced, snapping everyone out of their trance.

We maneuvered the canoe to the northern bank of the river, as Mr. Meek would have done on the Deschutes so many years ago. I jumped out and pulled it ashore. Emily could have made an easy jump onto dry land, but she had to make a big splash in about eight inches of water dousing us all. I unloaded her big oxygen tank and put it on the two-wheeled cart so she could pull it behind her.

"What now?" asked Tiffany as she disembarked.

"Now we search this whole bank for the next clue," I said.

We spread out in different directions not really knowing what we were looking for.

The mark below
The eyes of the owl

I was looking for rocks positioned in the shape of

an owl face or something of the sort. Nothing jumped out at me. We had been searching for about thirty minutes when Tiffany saw the first markings and called us over.

"Guys, look at this rock. There's a picture etched into it. It looks ancient," she said.

Sure enough there was an eight-inch-tall etching in a flat-faced rock that showed a man with a spear hunting a deer.

"Here's another one," Emily called from a few feet away.

The more we looked around, the more we discovered rock drawings everywhere we looked, some newer, and some ancient appearing.

"I think it's clear we're looking for a petroglyph of some significance," I said.

"How will we know which one is the right one?" asked Emily.

"Eh, I'm not really sure. Use The Force or something? I have a feeling it will come to us. Let's search," I said. What I really thought though was, *I hope it will come to us.*

It turns out, all over New Mexico there are rock drawings called petroglyphs that mean different things. They come from people tens of thousands of years ago, to Native Americans, to more recent hippie-graffiti. The problem for us was, and we hadn't figured this part out yet, how to pick the right one.

As it turned out, I had grossly overestimated our threesome's proficiency at cryptic petroglyph inter-pretation. Two hours later we were still combing the riverbank, searching for the right one. And mankind's second greatest enemy (doubt) was starting to invade my thinking. (His greatest enemy by the way is fear). *Maybe we were on the wrong bank? Maybe the "Meek" interpretation of the poem was wrong?*

We were facing obstacles unforeseen. First of all, the carvings while numerous were deftly hard to see in the bright direct sunlight. Often, if you thought you saw one on one of those flat gray basalt rocks, you usually had to wait until a cloud shaded the sun a bit then the contrast of shadow and light allowed the design details to pop.

And so this pattern went on and on repeating through the rest of the afternoon. One of us would find a drawing on a rock—call to the others—wait for a cloud to pass across the sun—study the art as a group—not agree on any unifying meaning—then scatter and search for the next glyph. We searched the whole day. It progressed to the point where I was about to have a major freak-out. Tiffany was able to talk me off the ledge.

It did, however, become apparent that our daylight was going to run out—and soon. The sun was dipping in the sky and the temperature had started to palpably drop. I pulled Tiffany aside and we agreed to camp for the night and resume our search fresh in the morning. We found a flat area sheltered on one side by the rock face about twenty yards from the water's edge. I gathered wood for a fire and the girls set up our tent. I had a flint and knife fire starter and sparked it over the kindling pile. We opened a dehydrated meal kit we'd bought from Gary which we put in a pot over the fire. I also knew how to make damper in the traditional Australian way. I showed Emily how to mix the flour, salt, butter, and water; knead it, and wrap the dough bun in foil. Then we buried it in the hot coals of the fire. An hour later we broke pieces off of the delicious bread with the crusty outside and soft doughy center. We drizzled each bite with a little local honey we'd bought in town, and it couldn't have been better. The taste and smell always reminds me of my time spent Down Under.

"Thomas, do you really think we're going to find the treasure?" Emily asked as we sat around the fire and gazed at the stars.

"I think we're within a thousand yards of it right now," I responded.

"The money will be enough to save me?" she asked.

"Yes, dear. Anyway, I think this journey may have

already saved us all."

"Come on. Let's get you to sleep," Tiffany said as Emily began to yawn. "I'll read to you and give you your shot." She took her by the hand into the tent. I gazed at an endless sky of stars, all millions of miles away, yet seemingly close at that moment and existing for my sole viewing pleasure.

The tent had been easy to assemble and the girls were inside. As the fire flickered, the stars glittered against the black backdrop of endless space-time. The river murmured peacefully to itself. I to in the smells. Ash from the burning pine wood. Damp mud from the nearby riverbank. Cool, clean air. And gold. I could smell the gold. I could sense its proximity. At some point, between the starlight and the hypnotic dancing flames of the fire and the water's hum, I fell asleep on the ground. I dreamt. I was running through the jungle. A jaguar was chasing me, bearing down on me. I carried a piece of green jewelry in my hand, and I sensed it had great value. The jaguar was gaining with every step. Soon it pounced, connecting with my left shoulder. It bit down and shook me violently. I tried to shake free. I raised the green jewel in my hand toward the monster. When I awoke, Tiffany was shaking my shoulder. I was shivering, uncovered in the cold. The frigid desert night was a stark contrast to its stifling sometimes choking midday heat.

I got to my feet. We stirred the remains of the fire and were fortunate to find some hot embers still smoldering at the bottom. I tossed on more logs and while I waited for them to catch, I breathed in the peaceful scene around me one more time before following Tiffany into the tent. It was after midnight already. Today was another day. Another chance. Another day I was grateful to have. I forgot about my dream as quickly as it had come.

The tent transformed into an oven as soon as the morning sun struck it and I awoke sweating. The girls were already awake and outside. I walked to the water's edge and knelt on my knees to wash my face.

Emily was sitting on a rock near the water's edge eating a granola bar about forty yards upstream. A big bank of cumulus clouds crossed the morning sun.

"Thomas!" she shouted. "You need to get over here and see this."

"OK, in a minute." I said, still splashing cold water over my face and neck.

"OK, but you're gonna want to meet Hootie's new friend," she responded.

"Really, and who is Hootie's new friend?" I asked absentmindedly as I tried glancing at a few rocks during the good cloud cover.

"The drawing of the other owl," she said.

I froze. The stanza replayed in my mind.

The mark below
The eyes of the owl
Under the call
Of the biG cat's wail

"Please show me, dear. Quickly. Before the clouds move on," I said, standing back up.

She walked over to a nearly flat, square rock about three feet off the ground, but kind of angled downward a bit. You wouldn't notice it if you weren't low to the ground and near the water's edge. An ancient glyph of a fat owl was carved into its surface, clear as day.

"Tiffany! We found something!" I called her over.

"What is it?" She asked as she came running up.

Emily pointed to the owl.

There was the owl, but what meaning did the rest of the stanza hold?

"'The eyes of the owl,'" I repeated. "Let's follow the bank that way, toward that rock cluster where the owl's eyes seem to be looking." We moved as a group along the shoreline about twenty yards to an odd rock cluster and began to study it. There were glyphs on several of the rocks, but the question was, which one pointed the way for us? I sat down near the river and replayed the poem in my mind. There had to be more, had to be something I was missing. I scratched out the randomly capitalized letters throughout the poem in the soft mud near the river's edge. They still didn't seem to spell anything.

O-T-O-R-O-M-N-G-O

I sat there in the mud staring at the letters. Emily walked over to see what I was doing. She didn't see yet that I had scratched letters in the mud. Her foot rested across one of the letters and obscured it. They now read:

O-T-O-R-O-N-G-O

"Emily you're the genius!" I exclaimed. "The 'M' was capitalized for 'Meek' because it's a proper noun. It isn't supposed to be in this part of the cipher. Without the 'M,' that's a word."

"Doesn't look like a word that I know," she said.

"It's not English," I answered. "It's Quechan. Incan. *Otorongo* is the Incan word for Jaguar," I said, quite unsure how I knew that.

We bolted over to the cluster of rocks and told Tiffany to look for a petroglyph of a jaguar. After a couple minutes, we found it, an ancient carving of a jaguar etched into the gray rock face.

Upon this discovery we all simultaneously looked "quickly down" to the base of the big rock and started digging. Tiffany unfolded the collapsible shovel strapped to her backpack and carved out a scoop of earth. Emily kicked smaller rocks away with her foot and I hauled off some of the larger rocks by hand. We quickly broke a sweat as the day warmed.

Once the top layer of rock had been removed, the soil was softer with more sand and digging became easier. After an hour of digging we stared at a three foot deep hole with nothing to show for it. Sweat covered us as the sun continued to beat down. Something wasn't right. I moved to the edge of the rapidly running water and splashed my face. I replayed the stanza in my mind. "Quickly down" seemed odd. There really hadn't been any wasted or unnecessary words in the poem so far. Why not say "look down?" Why say "quickly down?" The girls found the shade of an overhanging rock and rested there.

*Quickly down...Quickly down...*I'd heard that phrase before. About that time a hawk screeched and dove like a bullet to the ground on the hillside above us, snatching a desert mouse in the clutches of its talons.

It hit me like the hawk hit the mouse.

The angels came quickly down.

Shakespeare.

"Girls!" I called, jumping to my feet.

They had moved back to the hole and were about to resume digging.

"Hold up! The *angels* came quickly down. The vengeance came quickly down from above!"

Tiffany stood on the blade of her shovel and tossed another spade full of sandy soil to the side. "Tom, you've got heat stroke. Go lie down," she said without even glancing up.

"No, listen. We're searching in the wrong place. If he said look down, we'd want to dig down. He said look 'quickly down' which means we want to look *up*. You know why? Because, Mr. Dean's father taught high school English. All any boy has ever wanted in life is to make his father proud. And here is his chance. *King Lear*, Act 4, Scene 2, Line 48: 'Send quickly down to tame these vile offenses.' In the play the wrath of retribution came down from the heavens—down from above. He wants us to look up. He wants us to look up to the hillside."

"Wow," said Emily.

After the gravity of my words settled on us all we simultaneously looked "quickly down" which in this Shakespearean case, meant up. About two-hundred and fifty yards up the steep hillside from where we were standing, in the direction the jaguar was facing, just as I had predicted, was a thick clump of trees and a rocky outcropping.

We climbed. What I hadn't predicted though was the sheer and stunning beauty we beheld from up there. Once we made our way up the rock face and into the trees we found a rocky shelf about ten feet wide by six feet deep. If you sat on the shelf and looked out over the Rio Grande the view was spectacular. You felt like you were on top of the world. Below rumbled the river, and Sunset Rapids. Vast desert stretched out as far as you could see in every direction. Tiffany and I were absorbed in the view. Emily went around behind us and kept exploring. At the back of the shelf, behind a small debris field of light rocks, she found what seemed to be a small entrance to a cavern.

"Ahem. Are you love birds gonna kiss or are we gonna find some treasure?" Emily poked as she kicked away rocks from the cave entrance.

Tiffany's pretty cheeks pinked up as she blushed. The kissing would have to wait. We started moving rocks.

CHASQUIS

The Incan roadway system is a marvel, even in modern day. It's often compared in awe to the famed ancient Roman roads. The Incan roads were paved with stones and expansive. No corner of the empire went untouched by them. They spanned from coastal areas to jungles, from plains to mountains. Due to the empire's long narrow North-South orientation, most of the main highway-like roads were laid out in a North-South direction with smaller feeder roads branching off of the larger ones. Because the Inca never invented the wheel, there were no carts or wheelbarrows, so most of the roads were narrow and often steep because they were only needed for travel by foot. As a road wound up a mountainside, it often would switch back and forth on itself making many miles of paving work for the vertical ascent. Two famous roads in the empire were the lowland road that ran along the coast for over three thousand miles, and the highland road, also known as the Capac Nan which traversed four thousand miles of mountainous terrain. As travelers traversed the roadways, about every fifteen to thirty miles stood government funded rest stops called tambos. They were stocked with food and water, provided shelter to travelers, and were manned by caretakers.

Official government communications travelled along these roads, carried by relay runners called *chasquis*. *Chasquis* would run between *tambos* delivering messages that needed to be passed on to government officials, or even to the *Sapa Inca* himself. Ever played a game called telephone? The problem with this plan was that the Inca never developed a written language. So each message was passed along via word of mouth from one *chasqui* to the next until reaching the intended end receiver. As you can imagine, just like in the game of telephone, with that many handoffs of verbal information the message was sometimes flawed by the time it got to its destination.

Cura made it out of the deep jungle and turned onto the paved road toward the temple. With the firm stones under her feet and no underbrush to contend with her pace quickened even more. After about thirty minutes on the road she saw a figure up ahead running in the same direction as her. She could tell she was gaining on him though. As she got closer, she saw it was a *chasqui* government messenger, basically a professional male runner. She zipped past him and he stared at her, a befuddled look on his face.

She passed a *tambo*, not stopping for water. The road was winding up the mountain now and getting steeper with every hairpin turn. The air thinned the higher she climbed. She drank it in in ravenous gulps. Still she ran.

There! She could see the temple. She could hear the cacophony of the crowd. She could see the temple's peak rise to the level of the clouds. The sun shone close to its apex. The temple, clad in gold plating, reflected the sun's rays back into the crowds. It bounced a dazzling golden light in all directions. Manco was on the temple's high platform terrace with the high priest and the executioner. The priest was praying. There were two hundred thousand Incans between Cura and the base of the temple. She'd never get through the crowd in time. An idea struck her.

"Chasqui!" She screamed at the top of her lungs.

She screamed it again.

"*Chasqui*! I have a message for the high priest! *Chasqui*!"

A small aisle began to form through the crowd when the people heard her cries. She began to run toward the temple again, and was able to pick up her pace. She kept screaming as she ran.

At the temple Manco was laid down on the sacrificial stone. The executioner drew his knife in one hand as he held a cup in the other to collect Manco's blood.

The commotion in the crowd drew the priest's attention. He saw the aisle forming in the crowd and a small figure rapidly approaching the steps of the temple. He raised his hand and made a motion, signaling the executioner to pause. The girl was still screaming. "*Chasqui*," she rasped over and over again. Manco recognized her voice, and his already rapid heartbeat doubled its pace. Imperial guards stopped Cura at the temple steps.

"I am a *chasqui* and I have a message for the high priest," she said.

"Girls are not *chasquis*. They are not strong enough or fast enough," said one of the guards.

She let his ignorance roll off her back.

"One was injured on the road several miles back and I took his message and swore to deliver it," she lied.

"Tell it to me and I will take it up for you," said the guard.

"I swore to deliver it in person," she said. "It's a matter urgent to the fate of the empire. This message is from Huayna Capac himself. He will want it delivered in the promised fashion."

Invoking the name of the *Sapa Inca* got the guards' attention and the girl was allowed to pass. She sprinted up the steps of the temple. A wisp of cool wind blew in from the direction of the sea. It smelled of the open ocean. It smelled of salt.

Cura reached the platform at the top of the temple, made eye contact with Manco, and collapsed. When she awoke the priest was waving some scented grasses under her nose. He had also stuffed a wad of green leaves in the pocket of her cheek. She felt revived. She gave a slight nod of her head in thanks to the priest.

"Thank you," she said.

The priest nodded in return.

"I am Cura. I am of noble Incan blood." She held up the bracelet. "This bracelet has great spiritual value. The gods will be very pleased with it. I offer it up as a sacrifice to Illapa instead of this boy's life."

The priest took the bracelet from her. He twirled it in his hands, examining the way the light reflected off of it majestically. He looked at the girl and then back to the boy who was still lashed down to the sacrificial stone.

"This will augment our sacrifice," he declared. "You have done well to bring it to me."

He walked over the boy and placed the bracelet on Manco's wrist, wrenching his wounded shoulder as he did so.

"Illapa will like it." The priest admired it one last time before dropping the boy's wrist back to the ground. He then looked to the executioner and gave the order.

"Kill him."

"No!" screamed Cura. "The bracelet instead of the boy!"

"You're just a girl. And a stupid one at that. Decisions have been made," said the priest.

The executioner drew his knife again.

Cura stepped forward but the priest grabbed her by the upper arm and held her.

"It turns out we might also sacrifice noble blood today after all," he whispered to her.

Suddenly, a wind barreled in from the sea. It came on so strong that it nearly knocked them all off of their feet. The executioner was moved back and away from Manco three steps by the force of it. Black clouds hurtled with the wind and were carried eastward. Some also seemed to come straight down from the sky above. Inti was boxed out. It was dark. Then a layer of lightening covered the sky—and Illapa unleashed his pent-up rage.

The black clouds opened up a deluge. Lightening flashed, thunder rumbled, and two hundred thousand Incans rejoiced, their faces and hands pointed toward the sky. The black clouds surrounded them now as far as the eye could see. It was apparent that the whole empire was getting doused. The priest had let go of Cura. He and the executioner were looking up to the skies, dumbstruck. She ran to Manco and undid his bindings. They embraced for a long time, high on the temple in the middle of the storm—a storm the caliber of which had not been seen by anyone since Manco's ancestor first brought the bracelet to this same spot eight generations ago.

The Incan people danced in the streets and the human sacrifice was cancelled. The priest examined the bracelet on Manco's wrist closely one more time before mumbling something and excusing himself. Manco and Cura huddled together on the top of the temple for hours enjoying the show. At some point while up there they came to the decision to leave the empire in order to be together. If society's laws would not let them be together they would go out on their own. North or south was the question.

"We'll head in the direction of the next bolt of lightning," said Manco.

"Deal," said Cura.

The rain drummed in a continual rhythm. The sky was void of lightning for a moment or so until the brightest crack of the entire storm lit up the world just north of the temple.

"North it is," said Cura.

They left on foot the next day to start their new life.

A *huanacauri* draped the *Capac Nan* all morning the day they left. The bracelet dazzled brilliantly on Manco's wrist. In another display of spectacular timing Manco and Cura's decision to leave the empire and head north, again spared their lives. The melancholy end of a glorious empire was rapidly approaching to the sound of disease and Spanish horse hooves. *Sapa Inca* Huayna Capac died in 1526 along with over two hundred thousand other Incans of smallpox. The voided throne led to family feuding and a six-year civil war spawned by two of the former ruler's sons, Huascar and Atahualpa.

By 1532 Atahualpa had won the war and the throne but the empire was weakened by years of fighting and too vast to defend. At this point, by land area, it was the largest territory in the world.

The fate of the majestic Incan empire was sealed on November 16th, 1532 when the thin bearded Spanish conquistador Francisco Pizarro and one-hundred-ten men ambushed and kidnapped the

Incan king in the city of Cajamarca. Atahualpa's army of forty thousand warriors was defeated by a clever ambush, some trickery, horses, guns, and steel swords.

How far north Manco and Cura made it and how long they lived we'll never know for sure. But future discoveries would suggest they made it pretty far.

**** New Mexico 1990

A sixty-year-old Donovan Dean was tired but excited. The energy of the excavation had kept him going for forty-eight hours straight now. His team was wrapping up an archaeological dig in Southwest New Mexico that had yielded some extraordinary finds. There were spearheads and pottery shards that appeared to be Native American. But deeper digging had unearthed older relics that yielded evidence this had been a settlement for hundreds of years. Most puzzling, though, the craftsmanship and style of the pieces exhumed on the deeper levels of the dig seemed to be Incan in character, which didn't make any sense. Incan culture had no influence this far north, at least as far as we know. At any rate, the dig had been a success and the team was closing shop and packing up gear after a brief rain shower passed through.

"Look at how bright that rainbow is," a member of the team noted as she loaded a crate of gear into the bed of the pickup truck.

Donovan glanced over his shoulder and took note of a brilliant rainbow painted across the southern sky. He finished loading the last of the crates, got in the truck and started it. He took one last look around to see that no gear had been left behind. Off to one side, about five feet south of the last dig site, the sand glittered with all the colors of the rainbow.

That's an odd reflection, he thought. He turned off the truck and went to investigate, pulling a very special bracelet from the sand with a storied past and an unfinished future.

ONE WHO IS BOLD

Palpable excitement doesn't do justice to the emotions we were feeling. An entire chain gang tunneling under a prison wall for a taste of freedom after twenty years of incarceration couldn't have moved rocks as fast as we were slinging them. And then, before we knew it we were standing in an opening to a cave. We had to duck down at first but it soon opened up to become large enough to stand in. It looked to go back thirty or forty feet at least. Our flashlight-beams didn't reach the back wall from the entrance.

"OK, let's look around," Tiffany ordered, moving

ahead.

Once our eyes adjusted to the darkness, we realized the cave was a treasure as well. The inner walls were covered in petroglyphs. I'm no archeologist but they had to be ancient. Animal carvings, people, hunts. It was breathtaking. Toward the back of the cave we discovered a large pool of moving water about five feet across. It must have been spring fed, because the water had some motion to it, it wasn't stagnant. I couldn't tell how deep it was and I didn't have anything to probe it with. I sent Emily out to find a long stick. She returned and we probed it to be about four feet deep in most places. There was a spot near the middle that seemed to be slightly shallower.

Oh boy. Wet and cold, we'd been promised. I stepped down into the water and it must have been fed from some kind of a high mountain spring. *Cold cold cold!* I had to submerge most of my body to reach down and feel around on the bottom.

Wait, there it is! I felt a rectangular object. It was movable but heavy. I heaved it up out of the water and onto the cave floor above.

I couldn't bring myself to move again, and I forgot I was standing in close to freezing water as Emily worked the clasp on the chest. It was dark green. It was as described—ornate. Tiffany's hand trembled, her nerves given away by the fluttering beam of light from her flashlight. I reached out and touched her hand, steadying it. Emily tipped open the lid to the chest. Tiffany gasped and hugged Emily tight to her. Emily stuck her hand in the box. It was there. It was all there—ancient gold coins, gold nuggets, rubies, emeralds, diamonds, pearls, and the Incan bracelet.

"Holy shit," I said. "I mean I thought we'd find it, but to really find it...holy shit."

"Language," said Tiffany.

"Holy shit is right," Emily squealed, running ancient Spanish gold coins through her hands. That got a chuckle from us both.

The joy was short-lived though, because in true worst-timing possible, Hollywood-approved style, another voice echoed from the mouth of the cave.

HILLBILLY REVENGE

"Good job. Now carry the chest out here into the light for me and I'll make it quick and painless when I kill you all," the voice ordered.

Tiffany's light moved to the man's face. His nose was broken and poorly bandaged. He held a gun in his right hand and a rolled up map in his left.

"Girl's map fell out of her backpack at the shop yesterday. I appreciate that she had highlighted the route you all were taking. I just came following to even the score for my nose. I was just gonna rough you up a little. Maybe kill you, maybe not, but you found the treasure! Now I'll get to take it and kill you. Turning out to be a pretty good day after all." He motioned with the gun. "Swim-time is over. Get out of the pool, close the chest, and bring it to me."

His voice echoed a little in the hollowness of the cavern. I think it was the echo that gave me the idea. I pulled myself out of the water that I had somehow forgotten I was in. Emily closed the lid of the chest. When I knelt down to pick it up, I shot Tiffany a wink as the beam of her flashlight crossed my face.

"Let me bring the little girl out with me to see the view one last time? Let her take one last breath of fresh air, please?" I asked.

He turned around and looked out. I don't think he had noticed the view before, too preoccupied with his thieving and murderous plans. I motioned to Emily to come with me as I lifted the chest and headed toward the mouth of the cave. I tried to keep moving and talking the whole time to keep him distracted from my real plan. I pushed the chest out of the cave opening. Emily stood there with me, enjoying the view. There was a man with a gun next to us who had just promised to murder us all and she didn't seem a bit afraid. She stood there, her eyes scanning the horizon. I wedged the chest in the crevice between the mouth of the cave and the rocky shelf. He wasn't paying too much attention to me. He was watching Emily as she had taken a few steps out and was very near the edge of the ledge.

I summoned her back to my side at the cave entrance.

"Here, dear, take a deep breath. Get rid of this apparatus so you can get a good inhale of desert air," I said as I reached up and removed the oxygen tubing looped over each ear and laid it and the canister on the ground inside the mouth of the cave. She looked at me with a raised eye brow.

I kept talking, distracting him, while fiddling with the oxygen tank, "Hey buddy, we need less than half this money. That gold is worth more than two and a half million dollars. We need about eight-hundred thousand for the little girl's medicine—for her cancer. That's all we want. You can have the rest. You can have the other one point seven million to yourself. We'll even help you carry it out of here. You can have credit for finding the treasure and donating some of the money to help save her life. How's that sound?" I asked.

Dried crusted blood clung to the bottom edge of his poorly bandaged broken nose.

"You know what kind of a headache you wake up with after your nose is broke and you bout died of low blood sugar? I'll tell you. A bad one. Nah, I'll take option B. I'll kill you all and keep a hundred percent of the treasure for myself. Now get back in the cave."

"Thought that's what you might say."

I put my arm around Emily and we rejoined Tiffany in the back of the cave. I grabbed my backpack and used it as a shield between the gunman and ourselves. Tiffany did the same. We put Emily as far back in the cave as we could and I put my body between the shooter and the girls.

"Tom?" Tiffany's voice trembled.

"It's OK," I said searching for her eyes as best I could through the darkness, "Close your eyes and cover your ears."

Then, louder, to the gunman I added: "Get it over with you stupid hillbilly."

BLOOD AND SUNLIGHT

The explosion killed him instantly. His charred body was launched out over the ledge and down the cliff. The fire from the end of the barrel of his gun—the spark from the one and only shot he got off ignited the concentrated pure oxygen cloud he was standing in at the mouth of the cave and caused the explosion. When I was removing Emily's oxygen earlier, I was disconnecting the small oxygen tubing and opening the valve wide on the canister. I felt the heat on my back and the fire touch my neck. I fell backwards. My ears were ringing, and I was dizzy. The cave spun around me in large circular arcs. I tried to steady myself but the cave still spun. I looked at Tiffany.

"Are you alright?" I shouted. She didn't respond. My voice seemed slow and distant though. I shouted louder and shook her shoulder. She nodded.

I turned to Emily. She wasn't moving on the cave floor. "Emily, are you OK?" I reached out and touched her leg. It was wet. I groped the ground with my other hand for my flashlight to get a better look at the scene. When I found it, I flipped it on. Her leg wasn't wet. It was bleeding. Tiffany gasped.

"We have to get her into the light. I can't see well enough," I said as I lifted her small body and started toward the charred remains of the cave entrance. I laid her down in the warm sunlight of the rock shelf, and when I saw how pale her face had become, knew right away that we were in big trouble. I examined the wound. It looked like she was bleeding from the right upper leg, near her groin. I opened my knife and quickly cut her pant leg open. It wasn't a bullet wound; it must have been shrapnel. The bullet or the explosion must have ricocheted a piece of sharp rock that hit her.

"Tom?" Tiffany said.

I answered the one-word question without looking up. "It's the femoral artery. You can tell by the pulsating nature of the blood loss. The wound is too high in the groin for a tourniquet. She's bleeding so much because of the blood thinners. I have a multi-tool pocketknife in my backpack. Find it and open it to the needle-nose pliers."

I had to try to find the femoral artery and clamp it or tie it off. Problem was that sometimes, if it has been severed, it can contract back up into the pelvis a bit making it almost impossible to find.

Tiffany returned with the tool and I sent her back to the canoe for more oxygen mostly so she didn't have to watch this part.

"She'll need more oxygen soon. Hurry down to the canoe and get another cylinder. I'll find the artery and clamp it."

"OK," she said, then she bounded down the hill and over rocks like Rob Krar winning the Western States Race.

Emily was unconscious by now. I probed the wound. I searched it aggressively. Methodically at first, then deeper, then frantically, then fanatically. I couldn't locate the artery. I tried blind random bites of tissue with the pliers, hoping to get lucky. I asked for help from any deities who may have been watching or listening. The bleeding continued. The artery was severed and retracted into her pelvis.

When Tiffany got back with the oxygen I was covered in blood and holding pressure on the wound with both hands. My face communicated all that needed to be said. We placed Emily back on some oxygen. Her head rested in Tiffany's lap. As I look back now, I am grateful for her return to consciousness.

She awoke.

"It's cold," she whispered.

"Do you hurt, honey?" Tiffany asked.

"No."

"Thomas?" she asked.

"I'm here," I said. I already held her hand in mine.

"Don't let the dirt get in my mouth. I don't want dirt in my mouth."

"I know. I promise. Don't worry about that, dear. Just breathe."

I was also checking her radial pulse at the wrist against my blood-soaked fingertips as I held her hand. It was waning.

I leaned in close to her cheek.

"Chris and Kim are in a tight spot right now," I said. "How are they getting out of this one? Let's go somewhere. What book do you have? Where do you want to go? Just close your eyes and you can go anywhere. What do you think?" I asked.

She opened her eyes wider. She looked past me at the sun, the desert, the sparkling rocks, and the raging Rio Grande. Several moments passed before she answered.

"I don't want to ever go anywhere else," she whispered. "This is perfect."

A minute later her body went slack. The soft drumming of her pulse against my bloody fingers ceased.

The sun reddened and burned our skin. Our lips dried and cracked. We just lay there on the rock shelf in the desert sun. I don't know for how long. It may have been hours. Tiffany and I just remained lying there for hours with her body, not saying a word. Sometimes there aren't words for such a moment. Sometimes the moment is bigger. Sometimes the events of the world are so horrific as to be beyond the comprehension of the feeble human mind. And when faced with such events, the mind sits in stunned silence, unable to take another step forward on the cold un-empathetic earth. So we just lay in silence. Blood-soaked silence.

NO DIRT

I couldn't make myself get up. I wasn't thinking. Just being. Tiffany began going back and forth making trips to the canoe. I wasn't sure what she was doing. Eventually, I sat up enough to see that she was carrying the extra oxygen canisters from the canoe and stacking them in the cave. I lay back down. She kept working. I kept lying there. Thoughts of getting up came and went. She was in the trees on the hillside above the cave now gathering sticks and logs and bringing them into the cave. Tiffany knelt beside me. She did not look at me.

"We were her only family," she said. "She said she never wanted to leave here. Seems like a perfect final resting place after a great adventure. And she had that fear of dirt in her mouth. She never wanted that."

"Good final resting place," I said, finally realizing what Tiffany was planning. She stood and looked me in the eyes then extended her hand. I grabbed it and I was pulled to my feet with surprising strength. We gathered more wood and stacked a great heap of it in the center of the cave. We put an oxygen tank in the center and two others flanking either side. Together we gently placed Emily's body on the makeshift wooden platform. We tucked Hootie under her little arm. I closed her eyes for the last time. I kissed her forehead. Before opening the valves on the oxygen cylinders about a quarter turn, allowing for a long hot burn, and striking my knife against my fire-starter near the kindling pile, Tiffany gave a simple but perfect tribute.

"Emily. She was everything beautiful in life. She showed us how to live. She refused to let cancer define her life. We will see her again in sunny days, and flowers, and shapes in clouds, and anything beautiful this world has to offer."

I dragged the knife across the flint rapidly but it seemed to happen in slow motion. I saw a spark fall slowly, through the heavy air and land on the kindling.

It glowed red quickly in the oxygen rich air. Embers expanded into flames which then danced around the sticks and began to lick the larger logs. The oxygen sped the fire and heated it enormously. Soon it was too hot to even view the inferno from the rocky shelf. We watched the flames as long as we could and then began our retreat.

RETREAT

Tiffany and I held hands as we maneuvered our way down the hillside toward the water's edge and our waiting canoe. I knelt by the water and cleansed my hands for the first time, watching the blood run downstream and my hands turn pale again. I splashed my face and cleaned myself up as best I could. Tiffany untied our assailant's canoe which was ashore next to ours and waded out about waist deep in the water where she filled it with water and sank it, giving it a final shove toward the middle of the river in a downstream direction.

In similar fashion to how the treasure was brought in, we took it out. We emptied the contents of the chest into Tiffany's backpack and put the empty chest into mine. We loaded ourselves into the canoe and paddled back up the river in silence. Two lives this time headed up river instead of the three that had come down in the same boat two days before. Was it only two days ago? It felt like weeks. Night was falling and the desert sky glowed deep red. The air was cooling rapidly as the sun set. Despite our situation, the combination of peaceful evening sun, deep vermillion sky, and twisting river-cut canyon seemed to exude a soothing calm. When we reached the jumping-off point after our upstream paddle, we ran the front end of the canoe aground and Tiffany hopped out and pulled it up on land. She extended a hand to me and I took it and jumped ashore. We pulled the canoe further up and then placed our backpacks in the back of the Jeep. It was dark now. We hoisted the canoe onto the roof of the Jeep and strapped it down. She looked me up and down then took the keys from me without asking. She started it up and we pulled out of the lot.

"Wait," I said. "There by the road. That truck. I saw it at the outdoor gear store."

"He won't need it anymore." She paused for a second before seeming to think out loud, saying: "We could run it off a cliff nearby, or try to push it into the river. People probably overnight camp around here though and it may not be that unusual to have a vehicle stay in one place for a few days. Neither one of us has touched it at this point anyway.

"Let's just leave it," she concluded firmly, and drove us back toward town.

We reached the hotel without event. We waited in the Jeep for a good ten minutes on the chance anyone was following us. No other cars came near us and we didn't seem to have been followed.

"Tom," she said.

I was staring off into space. She took my hand and squeezed it.

"Tom, I know we've been through a lot today. But I have to ask you to get it together. I need you thinking about what to do next. We have over two million dollars in treasure in our trunk with no reasonable way to move it or convert it to cash, and we just left two bodies in the desert."

I nodded.

We went to my room. I was still shaken and numb. The fog that shrouded my brain was beginning to lift but it was still present. I was fiddling with a golf ball I had found in the Jeep. I hadn't looked at it. I was just tossing it back and forth from hand to hand.

Tiffany threw her pack on my bed. She bolted the

door. I sort of just stood there, tossing the ball around. She had brought a screwdriver from the Jeep. There was an access panel on the exhaust vent of the fireplace. Tiffany unscrewed and removed the cover and placed her backpack down inside. The other pack, the one with the treasure box in it, got placed under the fireplace itself, where the ash collection tray normally resides.

"I'm going to go shower. We'll figure out what to do in the morning after we've gotten some sleep," she said.

"OK, good night," I answered.

I closed the door as she retired to her own room. I flopped back on the bed and tossed the ball up toward the ceiling. As it paused at the apex, before the inevitability of gravity pulled it back toward my face, I was staring right at the logo of a barred owl. Then it hit me. Right in the face. I was too lost in a tornado of thought to catch it, and it cracked me right in the face. Served me right, but it also kind of woke me up. I ran out to the Jeep. There was a business card in there that I had to find.

BAT - PHONE: REPRISE

"Pine Valley Concierge."

"Yes, hello? This is Dr. Thomas Beck."

"Dr. Beck. How can I help you this evening?"

"You know who I am?"

"Of course, sir. It's a short list of people who have access to our services."

"Oh, OK. I'm in a bit of a pinch. I need a private jet pick up for two people in Taos, New Mexico."

There was a brief pause and some clicking of keys on a keyboard on the other end of the line.

"I see here there is a small airfield in Taos called

Taos Regional. Will that do, sir?"

"Yes."

"And when will you need pick up, sir?"

"As soon as possible."

"And what is the destination?"

"Anywhere but here. But we also will need to move some very valuable antiquities and jewels. We need to liquidate them discretely and quickly."

"I see, sir. Let me arrange the transportation and see about moving your valuables. I will message you back shortly."

"Thank you."

"Have a pleasant evening, sir. And thank you for being a friend of Pine Valley."

I hung up the phone and showered. When I finished there was a knock at the door. Tiffany was there. She wore only an American Aquarium t-shirt. Her jet black hair was wet and shining. She was radiant.

"I don't want to be alone right now," she said.

I let her in.

The concierge messaged me back with the details of our escape plan and I shared them with Tiffany as we lay in bed.

"We need to move this treasure—and fast. First of all, there are a great number of people who would prefer to just kill us for it. Second, if this becomes public knowledge there will be fights over taxes and whose land it was found on, and legal battles, and to hell with that noise. We're putting this money to good use. Third, we did kill a guy out there. He sort of killed himself with Darwinian stupidity, but we still don't want to deal with any of that heat."

"So, how are we moving it? How are we getting it out of here?" she asked.

"I have some friends. There's a plane picking us up in six hours."

KEEP IT

"Keep it."

It was a bucket list item. The tossing of the keys. There was a guy standing on the runway at Taos Regional airfield six hours later telling me I couldn't park my Jeep there. I'd always wanted to do like in the movies—toss my keys to someone and just say, "Keep it." As the off-white Beechjet Hawker 400XPR touched down nearby, I got my chance. Tiffany had never been on a private jet before. The pilot asked our weights. I warned Tiffany ahead of time to factor in our heavy packs that would not leave our sides during the trip. He sort of looked us up and down skeptically but didn't challenge our falsely heavy listed weights.

As luck or fate would have it, there happened to be an antiquities dealer of just enough questionable repute to deal with us at a current convention in Las Vegas. We were just over seven-hundred miles away. This was easily within the Hawker's listed range of 1,905 miles. And with her top speed of 518 miles per hour, this would be a short flight. We took off quickly after a fuel top off. The interior was plush. There was no attendant, but there was a bar. It was still dark as we lifted off and I looked out over the New Mexico desert. The sun was just beginning to pink the sky to our right. Tiffany opened her backpack on the seat next to her and we stared at the treasure for a bit. She then went to the bar, popped the cork on a bottle of Dom Perignon 2008, and poured two flutes.

I looked to her, surprised.

"Yeah, if I've learned anything on this adventure, it's that life's too short to not drink pristine champagne on a private jet. Cheers." She lifted her glass.

We toasted, sipped champagne, and stared out the window at the desert disappearing below us while the treasure sat silently on an empty seat next to us on our way to Las Vegas.

STOP AND SMELL THE FLOWERS

If you've never been to the Bellagio, I highly recommend it. Of all the glamour, posh, panache, and extravagance that is Vegas, the walk into the Bellagio is my favorite part. Past the fountains in front, Chihuly sculpture in the lobby, and then into the massive flower garden. I love the walk into the Bellagio—it's the smell. Tens of thousands of flowers in magnificent rotating arrangements continuously amaze and delight guests. Emily would have loved it too. And as I pondered that, it didn't make me sad. The thought of her enjoying this made me smile.

The casino had graciously sent two guards to escort us to our meeting when they learned of the value of our cargo. They met us at the airport. They were large shouldered and imposing looking. They wore gray suits. Our meeting was somewhere in the maze of secure underground rooms in the bowels of the Bellagio. We were supposed to enter through a side door and be rushed down a secure elevator to avoid the public eye and crowds. Much to the dismay of our escort, I insisted we enter through the front doors for the experience of the flower smells. I held Tiffany's hand in mine as we toured the enormity of the Bellagio flower garden with the public. Millions of dollars in treasure and ancient artifacts rode in our backpacks. Annoyed bodyguards trailed twenty feet behind us like chaperones at a junior-high dance. We bought espresso and French croissants near the chocolate fountain before heading down to the meeting room.

THE JEWELER

The jeweler was Austrian. He was polite. He was excited. He was impeccably dressed. Other than that he appeared to be about sixteen-years old.

With a slight accent he asked to confirm only that nothing we wished to sell had been stolen.

We confirmed that to be true, and he took us at our word.

We laid the items out on a large red cloth covered table that had been prepared for us. He looked at the enormity of the spread and stammered something in his native tongue. He took a note pad and a jeweler's loupe from his case and began his appraisals.

"Please make yourselves comfortable. This will take several hours," he said.

One of the casino-muscle that had escorted us from the airport came over and handed me two room keys.

"A suite was reserved for you by the gentleman who called to make your arrangements. If you would like to go shower and rest, we will stay here. Everything is safe with us here at the Bellagio, sir."

I looked to Tiffany and she shrugged.

"Sure," she said.

The "suite" was actually the Executive Parlor Suite. 2,500 square feet with its own pool table, media room, and bar. It was easy to get comfortable and clean up. We ordered a room service breakfast. A whole spread; muffins, breakfast breads, etc. We then looked at each other in our dingy camping clothes and agreed we felt underdressed. We went down to the shops and bought new clothes. Look good, feel good. After spending a couple more hours being fitted out to the nines, I got a tap on the shoulder and was notified that the jeweler would see us now.

The jeweler had been busy. He had numbered each piece of the treasure including the treasure box. Then he had created an itemized list of every piece, complete with description and valuation. In total, he estimated the value at three point six million dollars.

We settled on three million for the lot. It was to be a cash deal. And along with the deep discount and the cash came no questions.

"There is one item that has captivated me since I first saw it," the jeweler said as he picked up the bracelet from the table with great care.

Its once bright silver was tarnished but the turquoise inlay still sparkled.

"Do you know its history or origins?" he asked.

"I'm afraid I do not," I answered.

"I think it may be pre-Columbian," the jeweler continued. "If you don't mind, I have a client who's a wealthy collector and would go crazy for this piece. I'd love to purchase it separately from the other items. Not on behalf of my company but for myself and my client.

I hesitated.

"I'll overpay," he added quickly. "I appraised it at fifty thousand dollars. I'll give you twice that.

Tiffany stepped forward between us and shook his hand.

It would take him a day to get the money wired, he said. We had a suite and new clothes and we were now in no hurry. We were in no hurry to go anywhere for that matter and we stayed a few extra days. Four days later we left Las Vegas, again on the Hawker, this time carrying three point one million dollars—cash money.

DOCTOR - NOW!

"Doctor, they need you NOW! Hurry she's fully dilated and pushing!" The nurse barked at me through a cracked hospital room door.

"I know. I know. Guidewire is out. Flushing lines. I saw no PVCs on the monitor," I responded. I was placing a central line on an unstable patient at my new hospital. I was pressingly needed on the OB unit now though. I peeled off my operating gown and tossed it toward the rubbish bin as I maneuvered away from the sterile field and sidestepped my assistant.

"Stitch it in," I ordered on my way out the door.

"Me?" asked "boy medical student." He had a name. I was sure of it. He looked at me with wide eyes.

"Yes, you. You can do it. This the moment you've been waiting your whole life for, kid. And tell the nurse to give the blood and fluids we discussed right away."

"Sir, doesn't protocol say I should get a STAT portable chest x-ray to confirm the line placement before I tell the nurse it's okay to use it?" he asked.

"Everybody wants to be a cowboy, but nobody wants to do cowboy shit. He's dying, kid. You can save him or not. It's your call."

I was out the door and bounding down the stairwell before he could plead his objections to being left alone. I jumped out on the obstetric floor and sprinted down the hallway. Room seven.

"Doctor, here comes the head. Do you want to take over?" the gowned obstetrician asked me from the foot of the bed as I entered.

"Just do a good job," I said, leaning down near the head of the bed and taking Tiffany's hand. I smiled and kissed her forehead.

The cries of our newborn baby filled the room shortly after. They placed her in Tiffany's arms.

"Congratulations! It's a girl. What will you name her?" The nurse smiled down at us.

"Emily," her mom replied with a smile and a cathartic flood of tears. Some tears happy and excited about new times to come, some melancholy and longing for those times that had already been, but all born from a place of deep love.

EPILOGUE

As too often happens, Doxybutex was a flop. It was pulled from human trials shortly after they began, ironically for the unforeseen side effect of uncontrollable blood thinning leading to hemorrhage. As painful as it was, Emily had no more time left, whether she'd made it out of that desert or not. The treatment would not have done her any good. The research for pediatric cancers was not there because the funding was not there. Unfortunately, it's still not where it needs to be even today.

The nice part about being a physician is that there

has always been, and will always be, demand for services. I got a new job with one phone call. Tiffany and I were married. Mr. Smith survived my version of halfway-house cardiac electrotherapy and we are now good friends. I'm fortunate enough to still be on his invitation list to Pine Valley about once a year. It's the honor of my life and I love it.

As far as the treasure, we split it evenly three ways. One million dollars to each of us. Emily's third was divided as we thought she would have wanted it: half to the Caroline Symmes Cancer Endowment, and half to the Audubon Society under the simple donor name of Hootie. Tiffany paid off her existing school loans and paid for law school. She was also able to pay for college for her younger twin brothers with half of her share. Her other half also went to the cancer endowment. I did something against my better judgment, but something I've never been able to help. I gave half of my share to John-Boy for the hedge fund. Time will tell. I made a much better decision with my other half and our total donation to the Caroline Symmes Cancer Endowment totaled one point six million dollars. For some inexplicable reason we had felt compelled that all of the one hundred thousand dollars from the jeweler for the turquoise bracelet go to a good cause. We hadn't touched any of it.

*** Tennessee—Present Day

Sarah McClain was a molecular genetics graduate student working on a small cancer research project out of Middle Tennessee State University. She did not stand a chance to get funding for her research.

"It's just too competitive this year. Your project is a nice idea but it's not going to lead to any change," is all she kept hearing.

She had submitted the application paperwork anyway, but only held out a thread of hope for funding. Sharks are notoriously resistant to cancer, it's thought. Her project involved snipping shark DNA and encoding that into a virus, then using the virus as a vector to target cancer cells in mice.

She was packing up for the day and cleaning up her lab. Her professor walked in holding a letter.

She opened it and he read over her shoulder "....unexpectedly more funding this year than anticipated.....awarding you a research grant in the sum of $100,000."

Somewhere in the Swiss Alps, a wealthy European antiquities collector stood in awe under a rainbow. The bracelet on his wrist was doing incredible things with the light.

CAROLINE'S STORY

Cancer is a terrible thing. Pediatric cancer is a particularly horrific subset that no child, parent, or family member should ever have to endure or experience. It's one of those things that we, as human beings of any race or background from across the planet, uniformly wish did not exist. Unfortunately, that is not the case as it stands today. Sources quote only about four percent of federal funding for cancer research is dedicated to childhood cancers, yet the burden for us all is real. Each day the United States experiences about forty-three new pediatric cancer diagnoses and eight hundred new cases are reported world-wide each day. That totals more than three hundred thousand new cases per year worldwide and that is, without question, an underreported number. And when discussing diseases that kill our children, cancer is reported as the leading cause of death by disease in American children at a price of 1,800 lives per year.

All hope is not lost, however. Brilliant people are actively dedicating their lives to make sure the future tells a much different story. One where childhood cancer is a disease of the past. The Caroline Symmes Children's Cancer Endowment has pledged to raise money for childhood cancer research to help make that dream a reality.

Caroline Symmes was five years old when cancer ended her life. Out of her tragedy, this foundation was born to fund research and inspire hope in future pediatric patients and their families.

Caroline was three years old when she was diagnosed with Wilms Tumor disease. As the most curable type of kidney cancer in adults and children, Wilms Tumor has a ninety-percent survival rate. But Caroline had a very aggressive tumor, and with so little in the way of research for pediatric cancers, her physicians quickly exhausted their options to treat the disease.

She never cried or complained. With an old soul and a big smile, she lived her short life to its fullest.

Caroline lost her future not because of a lack of care or resources, but because of a lack of funding for pediatric cancer research. The Caroline Symmes Children's Cancer Endowment is the gift she leaves behind, one that strives to ensure every child with cancer can live with hope for a bright future of their own.

Half of any money raised from the sale of this book will be donated to the Caroline Symmes Children's Cancer Endowment to fund pediatric cancer research. If you would like to join me, learn more, become involved, or donate please visit: carolinesymmes.org.

Made in the USA
Las Vegas, NV
08 December 2021

36685077R00177